2 Ennerdale Drive:

unauthorized biography

2 Ennerdale Drive:

unauthorized biography

Rosa Ainley

Winchester, UK
Washington, USA

First published by Zero Books, 2011
Zero Books is an imprint of John Hunt Publishing Ltd., The Bothy, Deershot Lodge,
Park Lane, Ropley,
Hants, SO24 0BE, UK
office1@o-books.net
www.o-books.com

For distributor details and how to order please visit the 'Ordering' section on our website.

Text copyright Rosa Ainley 2010

ISBN: 978 1 84694 560 1

A CIP catalogue record for this book is available from the British Library.

Design: Stuart Davies

Printed in the UK by CPI Antony Rowe
Printed in the USA by Offset Paperback Mfrs, Inc

Image credits:
© TfL from the London Transport Museum collection, page 38
Museum of Domestic Design & Architecture, Middlesex University, page 51
Evening Standard, page 105
All other images from the author

Due effort has been made to trace copyright holders of material that appears in this book. If we
have been unable to reach you, please contact us so that the situation can be rectified in
future printings.

The existence of some of the people in this book is a matter of historical record, as are some
events described here; others have been created to serve the purposes of the author or those
of the narrator. None of the characters is identical with anyone, living or dead. The result of
historical figures mixing with fictional characters is fiction.

We operate a distinctive and ethical publishing philosophy in all
areas of our business, from our global network of authors to
production and worldwide distribution.

CONTENTS

'A house contains a body of images that give mankind
proofs or illusions of stability.'
Gaston Bachelard, *The Poetics of Space*, 1994

Acknowledgements

First and always, I want to thank Jo Henderson who makes every-thing possible.

Many people have contributed to the development of this work. Excerpts from the book were delivered as readings at the Archi*text*ure conference at University of Strathclyde in April 2008, and at the Writing Gender and Space conference at Warwick University in March 2009. I am grateful to the organizers, Craig McLean (Strathclyde) and Charlotte Mathieson and Arina Cirstea Lungu (Warwick).

I am indebted also to staff at the archives I visited in person and online, especially to Maggie Wood and Zoë Brealey at the Museum of Domestic Architecture at Middlesex University. Tim Brittain-Catlin and Elain Harwood made useful suggestions for readings on suburbia. Among the readings and comments that helped shape the book, those from Katherine May and Vanessa Norwood were particularly useful on the opening sections.

Working with Kirsty Hall was an invaluable process that deepened my understanding of what I was trying to do and why, with this book and beyond.

Heartfelt thanks go to Janet Harbord and Sarah Turner for support, enthusiasm and contributions to my thinking on the project; to Pekoe Ainley, Tim Holmes and Charles Mowbray for feeding me with stories, contacts, genealogical information and materials; and to Sarah Cooper, who kept asking 'when can I read it?'

Chapter 1

Telling tales

Exhibit 1: Directory portrait

I'm holding a borderless black and white photograph, a bit battered round the edges. It looks like a working print even though it's perfectly black and white, from the exact white rendering of one man's hair to the dense blackness of the other's. The graininess of the image is a good match for their lived-in, blemished, lined faces. On the back of the print is a badly inked stamp impression of a photographic studio credit. The format is landscape but it's a portrait, actually a double portrait. Do two portraits make a landscape? Something else, other than the format, gives it an unusual look: it's not a regular size for photographic paper. It's 8¼ x 11½ inches. That's a size that works better in millimeters: 210 x 297mm or A4, in other words. The dimensions are

1

those of a paper size and while the actual dimensions are not much changed, it makes a lot of difference. The picture looks strange because it's not 8 x 10, a more regular size for a photograph.

A young man stands behind an older one. Both men look into the camera, a quarter turn of the shoulder away, so neither is full face but almost the whole of both faces can be seen. They must be father and son. The left side of the younger man's face is in shadow, the older man's much less so. The old man's lips are slightly parted and there's something of a gleam around the eyes. His companion is not twinkly; the smile, almost there, is not quite comfortable.

Father and son: the relationship inscribes particular readings on to the image. Son, above and behind, looks taller than Father. Son is set to take over from his father and can afford to stand in the hinterland a while yet. Son is slipping into a position of caring for his father, of looking out for him, of nurture, of responsibility towards the older man who is closer, much closer as it turned out, to death. The contrast of the son's dark jacket and the open top button on the light shirt with Father's pale jacket and dark shirt, speaks of a rejection of old ways, of his father's ways. He's moving on to the new. Such a direct, total contrast between them makes it a connection of call and response in the end: an echo, rather than a separation. The older man can afford to be relaxed and smiley; his son is in position behind him to catch him should he falter. Perhaps, you might think, he has nothing else to prove, and his son is getting ready, positioning himself to take on the role of patriarch.

Neither man is particularly well groomed; they haven't brushed their hair or dressed up in their best clothes. Father, white-haired and going bald, has a tuft at the front and a stray strand of hair falling on to his forehead. His beard, which rather suits him, could be saying 'salty sea dog' or 'academic'. He's wearing a linen jacket over a corduroy shirt with the top button fastened but he doesn't look very buttoned up. Son is wearing a tweed sports jacket and a cotton shirt of a tiny check, open at the throat. His abundant hair and eyebrows are very dark.

Any viewer of the photograph would assume they are father and son, and they could be, just. Their ages make this possible; more than 20 years separate their births. Father's older daughter, The Sis, is older than the younger man. He is her uncle and mine too. The men in the photograph are brothers, not father and son. They are two of the sons of Mr Henry Ainley, the actor. Two portraits make a landscape of family but this is a landscape of brothers.

The two brothers are almost, and presumably deliberately, negative impressions of each other. Who dressed them? They both look very much themselves, each dressed in their own style but they surely didn't fall into the negative/positive, black/white correspondence by accident. They look on the move, like they're going somewhere. There's an air of expectancy about the photograph, as if, posed and poised as the image is, they really were just captured and temporarily stilled, consigned to print on their way to somewhere else. There's a closeness, they're at ease in this proximity. From different generations and different mothers from different continents and backgrounds, it's a big bridge to cross. For all that, quite a brotherly relationship existed between the two, so I'm told.

The older more established brother, Richard, my dad, looked out for Antony, his younger sib, as he would have called him. Maybe something of a mentoring role was being played out, given that they shared a profession as well as a father, or perhaps brotherly competition arose over these things. Maybe they were competitive instead about their domestic lives: one lived with his own family and the other still lived at home with his mum, where he continued to live until first her death and then his own. Antony is standing back, receding into the background, disappearing into his jacket, gallantly allowing his older has-been brother the glory of front position. Antony might have been positioned as taller, the better to be able to take care of his older brother, though I would have been certain that my dad was the taller one. Certain that is, until I realized how big and safe my dad loomed for me when this photograph was taken.

This little brother was born when Richard was a young man of 22. Already making a mark on the London stage and screen, he was about to decamp to Hollywood to make films and, so the story goes, walk Merle Oberon's dogs between pictures. His left side is partially hidden in the photograph, and hidden too, though this was increasingly less visible, is an oddly shaped head, as well as a metal plate in his skull and partial paralysis caused by a war wound. And was the younger brother able to help when his older brother returned war-damaged with 20-odd film roles to the good? How would he? He was a teenager. Antony must have been about 13 when his older brother came back from the US. It strikes me how much deeper this distance stretches. If they hadn't already met by then, their father was unable to introduce them as he had died in 1945. Fifteen years later I appear, and I don't remember there ever being a time when Antony wasn't around, part of the family, bombing over in his Mini from his house in Colindale, being Uncle Ant. There was nothing half about his brotherness by then.

This is the only photograph I own of the two of them together and it's clearly some kind of promo portrait taken in a studio: brothers playing actors off duty, or actors playing brothers. It's a photograph of who they are when they're not playing anyone but themselves yet are still on display for work. It's a publicity shot of the acting Ainley brothers; to what end and with what purpose in mind? Their careers, both in the same profession, both established, were widely divergent. They never worked together but perhaps this was a plan for the future.

This is the only one I own but more than that, it's the only photograph of them together that I have ever seen. I wonder about the other photographs of them that must have existed. A publicity shot might be selected from a roll or three, and more than one would be printed up to compare before a final decision was made. Outside the studio my dad would be behind the camera and seldom its subject. What's missing is the fruit of those occasions when an unknown member of the public is pressed into service: 'Excuse me, would you mind taking a picture of my brother and me? Thank you.' My dad was a prolific photographer and often carried our Kodak Instamatic around in his pocket, which was a much more bulky and heavier undertaking than it is in these days of wafer-thin technology.

Maybe my dad only liked having his photograph taken for work, and shied away from appearing in personal pictures. He may have become sensitive about being photographed, with age or injury or both. I remember another one-off picture of him in my family collection and I wonder if this uniqueness is characteristic. This time it's me who is in the frame with him. It's a photograph of us two together. Just me and my dad, that's special. The two of us are sitting outside somewhere, in Eastbourne or Seaford I'd say, for no reason other than my parents liked to visit the English south coast and many family trips there are documented through the pieces of furniture bought as well as by photographs. How this picture pleased me. I remember how unusual it was for us to be center stage in a picture, with no one else crowding us out. Well, me. He didn't get crowded out. He took up space, he got noticed. I know why there are few pictures of the two of us: because we were often together when everyone else was out at work or at school and he was the one with the camera. I don't remember any other photographs of us: of me by him, yes. I have a full cache of memories of us two being together but this picture is a precious document, a back-up, if you like. I still like to have the evidence. I must have filed it away somewhere carefully because I don't know where it is but I know I'll never lose it.

The brothers' plan for the future could have included using this image in *Spotlight*, the actors' directory. *Spotlight*'s website mentions Laurence Olivier, Boris Karloff, John Gielgud and Vivien Leigh as examples of the caliber of artists who appeared in the early editions. The directory was first published in 1927, with 236 artists including Henry Ainley. He is found in the Feature men section 'applied to artists who play star roles only'. There is no photograph. I thought it was absent because he wouldn't have needed one by that stage, his face was well known and his reputation preceded him. In fact promo portraits were still relatively rare in the early editions of *Spotlight* and only became standard in the 1960s. No image then, but unbelievably his phone number is included: KEMsing 1Y3, wherever that is. *Spotlight* was then published quarterly at a charge of 2/- (10p), post free but not available for public sale. By the time the autumn 1933 edition appears Henry's phone number is no longer included and Laurence Olivier features in the Juvenile men section. No picture for Olivier either but a Kensington phone number, which makes me realize that KEMsing must be a typo. It's Kensington, surely. It's a likely place for Henry to have lived too, smart and close enough to where he worked in the West End. Since 2007 *Spotlight* has included dancers, and listings for agents, casting rooms, studios and casting services. It doesn't allow 'duos' though, except for presenters and in the Children & young performers section where siblings and family groups can appear together. Old siblings need not apply.

The picture of the two brothers has been pinned up, probably by me. Each corner has one or more drawing-pin holes punched through it. Amid all the fingerprints across its surface (and they're likely to be mine too), I can see that the print has been 'spotted' with Spoton, tiny pecks from a fine sable brush with a range of dilutions of blue-, brown- and green-black to remove the appearance of marks. Fixating on the technicalities of the photographic is one way of reading the image and one way of keeping back the strangeness. Every photograph is about an absence, a stand-in for a memory; what is it about this one? A portrait photograph is always a (semi) permanent trace of a human being, a memorial to a moment. The shutter moment is over of course, and the brother moment too, since both men in the photograph are dead, but their absence is an almost palpable presence.

For actors and criminals, as Walter Benjamin has it, a photograph establishes an identity. It unmasks them, if an actor can ever be unmasked. This photograph pictures them as I last knew them and so they are fixed, mentally and chemically, as I will always only know them. I know too that this is only a smear of their identities. For me, the image transmutes into something beyond three-dimensional, almost interactive, as though I can step across time and through paper into the image, into that space. I would feel the stuff of their jackets and shirts, which is rendered so texturally in the image. I can almost feel the pressure of their arms around me. The magic of this image extends to the quality of its transport, its power to allow what Roland Barthes calls the fantasy of reversal. Photography can appear to unbind from the usual rules of time and space, and I can choose to fall for it. They can step out of the frame, back into an embodied real-time existence and carry on with their business, wherever it was they were going. It sounds as though I'm trying to un-dead them, which I suppose I always am. The present of this image becomes something of my past. In this present their past becomes something I can mess around, play rough with.

The more I look, the more I see, the more I make up, the more I toast the skill of the photographer. Two sides, same coin, each with their own patch, operating in their own sphere, no competition (I'm happy to make it my business to believe), no territorial dispute but so joined, so attached. Did they have this picture taken as a public statement of their brotherness, because it hadn't happened much in the usual way when they were growing up? We're two brothers, look at the picture and count us. We can fit into that category, thank you. Look at us, we're brothers! Perhaps they knowingly played the roles of father and son to each other as well as to their audience in this composition, both seasoned professionals and both robbed of the chance to explore fully in their lives the child portion of the father/son dyad. They could play this one out on a more public stage than the domestic, which was another one they never shared.

There's no knowing what the space of the portrait was. It's no space, a blankness of studio with a backsheet pulled down to simulate a space, and a fraction of time on an unknown date. The photograph is a fragment of their story, of their lives, of the life they shared. It's a proof for themselves of their status. It's a proof for me that I can read into as I please and I have, with a little help from a privileged position. There might be no directory that can contain them (aside from the entrapment of the combined direction of the photographer, their own sense of performance, and now mine) but they wanted it marked down, so that there would be no misunderstanding. I wonder which directory they made this picture for, to whom this information would have mattered anymore. It's clear, and touching, that it never stopped mattering to these two. That they were their father's sons is incontrovertible and forever inscribed at the head of anything either of them ever did; that they were brothers was a choice they were in a position to make. They fit, partially and fleetingly, into very many categories but together they make a single unit of their own.

'Oh darling, I'm so sorry.'

That was the first thing she heard as she picked up the phone that evening. The story opens with the flurry of phone calls that herald news, either good or bad. The first call came earlier in the day from 2 Ennerdale Drive. But she didn't get that one.

'Oh darling, I'm so sorry.'

Her sister kept saying it, as though The Sis herself was somehow responsible, as though the dead man had been an especially close relative, as though she had been in touch with him. She thought balefully that her sister must be talking about some other kind of family who enjoy fond and regular contact, outside of significant events.

She wondered if her sister wasn't expressing regret for something entirely different. Theirs is a family that does not know much about its other members. The family didn't like to pry, that must be it. Not that they didn't want to know, you understand, but you could never be sure what you were getting into. They embraced the pretence that there's no need to know, that their late-bohemian, (practically) anything-goes setup of a family doesn't need any further reassurance beyond what someone is actually like. But it's better not to ask, still. If you weren't there and haven't been told, perhaps you weren't meant to know and it all sounds a bit tricky anyway. What was it that happened to her again? And what about the youngest? Right. Was it a breakdown? Is that why he gave up the film career? Why did she never leave home? How come he didn't ever go back? Ah, open verdict. And how well did that one know his dad? Or, even, how well did that one know her uncle? Not very well. Not very well at all. Not at all. I'm getting there.

Pregnant pause: all that lack of information has to sink in, to settle somehow.

There was another call from 2 Ennerdale Drive. It was about Uncle Ant's funeral. She didn't get that one either. The second call was to Mrs A, her brother's ex-wife, whose number, once theirs, still sat in Ant's address book. Its pages hadn't seen much updating. Her brother had passed the news on as soon as he heard, he said; he'd had a call. It hadn't occurred to her at the time; no one likes to own up to the ignominy of being relayed information by the ex, with its pull of feelings more potent probably than those about the death of an uncle. Much later she understood that Mrs A had phoned her erstwhile husband to armor herself with foreknowledge about who else was coming; and Mrs A was the sole person who shared their name to attend the funeral.

Adrenalin was singing in her system by the time she finally spoke to The Sis. She had spent the whole day busily not phoning, not wanting her sister to be upset, not wanting to be the one to remind her sister that her contemporaries were old and dying. She imagined she was being helpful, pretending to know how someone else will feel, trying to avoid being the bearer of bad news, pretending to be selfless. What did she think she was doing? And The Sis already knew.

Her sister made the call.

'Oh darling, I'm so sorry.'

The Sis said again the words that might be better directed back at herself, since her loss sounds the sharper, and her usually so stalwart. It isn't only because it's on the phone or because she's just picked up the call that she doesn't know whether The Sis was making a belated vocalization of condolence for the loss of other shared connection, long gone. Can't tell, couldn't ask. Someone was in shock, by the sound of it.

There's another few phone calls yet. I'm getting there. Several weeks later she was sitting in a noisy restaurant when Mrs A called. She was busy making sheep's eyes at her new darling so she didn't hear the phone ring, wouldn't have picked up if she had. Mrs A left a very long message about this and that, the funeral and 'Poor Tom', the brother she didn't marry, whom she is threatening to contact to offer her support. She's been through some dark times herself and she knows how it is. Poor Tom indeed. Deaths in the family often have the effect of pulling an unraveled net back into shape, but Mrs A never was in her social circle, and there's not much family to be part of. It's only a name, and anyway it's hers. Tom has excised himself from the family story for the last 15 years, rubbed out his trail. He's not the first family member to be on the run from the long arm of family. Last known address – blank. No one has even an out-of-date number for him, or knows if he has a phone. His absence is clear and clean and total, very different from the busy unavailable tone that everyone plays from time to time. 'So you haven't heard from The Brother?', the refrain runs through conversations. Then there's herself: open, honest, present, and straightforward as the day is long. Of course.

I can give you some facts. Two hours before the funeral was due to take place, a phone call from her brother informed her that Ant, an uncle she hadn't seen for some 20 years, had died. She was more than two hours distant in travelling time and immeasurably far from covering the time needed to come up with a reaction to a loss almost theoretical so she couldn't go to the funeral, and nor did any of her siblings. The next day she managed to speak to Fred, Ant's brother, and to his daughter Catherine. Strictly speaking, Ant ('Tony' to everyone outside her immediate family) was her half-uncle, sharing a father but not a mother with her father, although there had been nothing half-about his uncleness either when she was a child. Fred shared a mother with Ant but not a father, so she was not actually related to Fred, it's true, but in a family like this one such slender connections become standard. Unusually for the time, we jumped the cracks of more regular family relationships and chose to ignore the unnecessarily conventional. The biological does not have to be the imperative.

• • •

It was Fred, the dead half-uncle's half-brother, who told her a little of the story of no.2, the house where the two of them grew up, the house she has always thought of as Ant's. Where does he come from this uncle brother son? It's not until they die that there's time to wonder who people are. Almost 50 years after he emigrated, Fred returned to an England he barely recognized to clear and prepare for sale a house that no longer had any of his family to fill it. Their 80-year occupancy is at an end. She's taking herself off to Ennerdale Drive in Colindale to see the house and to discover more about Ant, more about all of them maybe. This is the site where Ant played out his private life, so checking out the neighborhood is a start. There's a clutch of stories here already that might add up to something. There's a body and more than a few missing persons. There are suspects and accessories; there are motives, perceived or concealed. She has her suspicions. The leads may amount to nothing more than a portrait of a pair of dead brothers in the theater and a scene of no crime in particular but that's not how she sees it. Something tells her this house and this family will be good for a story or two. This is a story that needs a detective and she can play the part, she'll take it on herself. She can generate as much mystery and confusion as the case demands, with exhibits for evidence. She's setting herself up as investigator. No shot rang out in Ennerdale Drive. That doesn't mean nothing happened.

She's a detective hunting down a version of a family story starting with some brothers and an empty house. No crimes are on her books. Hardboiled isn't where she's trying to be, she's a detective trying to expose absences, missing persons, dead people. Nothing beyond the call of duty there, it's all in a day's work. She needs to know: what's the story? There's no trail so far but the one she's laying herself and there's no evidence but hearsay, photographs and anything retrievable from digital or human memory banks. But that's already a lot and it's enough to stand up in this court. She's a detective on a mission to put together the people hiding behind the curtains and people in the pictures, or even just to find the pictures she needs to make the case. That would be a good start. It's said, by Walter Benjamin again, that without photography the detective story could not have come into being, because a photograph can pin down the identity of its subject. Of course a photograph can do no such thing, she thinks, anyone knows that. Photography can, with prior knowledge, confirm that the image represents an identifiable scene, person or item. That's all it can do. Even with sophisticated disguises or plausibly documented false names, witnesses and diligence will lead to the pay off eventually. At least that's how it happens in the stories. Photographic evidence in detective stories and elsewhere can tell a truth of sorts then. It's never the whole story. A portrait photograph can be said to be without question a likeness of its subject, for instance. This is him. Publicity stills and press reports, received wisdom and footnotes are the sources of information to be amassed by this detective. It's all highly suspect but she'll get to the bottom of the available material so far. 'Beyond circumstantial' describes the status of most of it. She'll have to find the material she needs, that's her job. Licensed only by the imperative of her own desire and curiosity, she's the detective, and she's the spieler, the shapeshifter, the all-seeing she. So she says.

She shares a few characteristics with some of those other detectives she reads about: personal eccentricities; awkward, privileged interest in the 'case'; a tendency to make herself the story; and a need for suspension of disbelief. She has to move between this work role and family, find both within her at the required times, different sides of herself. She shares with the other detectives too the compulsion to investigate the private through the public. She could toy with the maladies befalling the detective in fiction: among them, heartbreak, loneliness, cynicism, fatigue and alcoholism. What she doesn't share with those other detectives: she doesn't have a sidekick, there's no name stencilled on a glass outer door of her office, and no bottle of bourbon in the filing cabinet.

A sole practitioner in the grip of an obsession, she's one of those detectives who has to spy for no money. Nothing and nobody to win, so no fee payable. This is the job as this detective sees it: she has to track down the evidence about this house and who lived here in whatever form she can find it. She will be reading imprints in houses, the pattern of bricks, the lay of the land and the light on the paper that made the photograph in order to translate signs and read into them what she needs to find there so that she can put together her detective's tale. The skill of the detective as she sees it is in the process of making paths, fashioning them into routes of significance, checking the boundaries between interior and exterior. Her role as detective involves making an attempt to be a panoptic beacon to illuminate and magnetize information. It's about knowing what to make of what is visible, effecting a transformation to see what's missing: a person, an object, a space, an idea. Making fragments into stories, putting pictures together into diagrams and extracting significant data from them, she'll have to stay with the job until a blur of identification and a shiver of awareness rises out of a mess of methodical scrutiny and dreamy surveillance, professional and personal.

Her gaze as detective takes in landscapes from the city to the hallway, suffocating or alluring, desolate or nurturing. Feeding the need to shift in scale repeatedly from micro and macro, from forensic examination of trace indentations in cushions to scanning the view, poring over street layouts and connecting the dimensions together can be sickening. The detective scales up the aperture, winds it down to take in the house next door, the street, the neighborhood; then narrows it again for the spotlight on the corner.

Each clue edges her pursuit onward, each speck of a sighting appears to have the answer, the clear view of what it is that she's looking for. *This* will be the key, *this* is the missing piece that will make the picture readable, lay out flat the entire story like a neatly set table. The revelation, the lost object identified and found, impossibly, will knit in every loose theme. Ah, but that kind of resolution would leave her stripped of dreams and dead and her an out-of-work detective. None of these leads ever keep the promise with which she imbues them, and so she's left instead alive and half-asleep and still in the job.

She doesn't have to travel far to look for representations of evidence in this job either in geography or cyberspace: Bristol to Stratford; Richmond to Olympia; Colindale to the West End, to Greenwich, to Kent. She could widen the scope of the inquiry, make it her life's work, the unsolved case turns into the one that forever haunts every retired investigator. For today, she's still on her way to Colindale, clunking along on the Northern Line, garnering a taste for where it all happened, the private life of the public brother in the picture. Maybe if she knocks on the door, someone will allow her to see inside the house one more time, just to see if she left any memory there.

Three stops before Colindale, at Golders Green, the train line emerges from the tunnel and turns into an overground train, a sure sign of crossing into suburbia. The train skirts past the backs of suburban villas in various shapes, the rear ends of many lives, past the red roofs of Hampstead Garden Suburb and on to Brent Cross, the place that's named for a shopping center and which isn't in Brent. The early-twentieth century Arts and Crafts houses and the 1970s mall are left behind as the train approaches Colindale, all 1980s-pastiche housing and urban fringe industrial buildings. The tube station is beneath a dull, brick building housing the National Blood Service, where a row of shops makes a small parade. Short runs of dead-looking terraces are interrupted by ever-diminishing small businesses. It's quiet even though the traffic's noisy. Nobody on the street hardly and nobody talks. Sullen London. Endless cafés and some of them busy. Not much in the way of life here.

She came here to immerse herself in local color and it's dirty mushroom. Once, it may have been possible to believe wholeheartedly in the myth that suburbs are about the desire to live in leafy residential areas designed to ensure the privacy and safety of the family. The evidence would make that hard to hang on to here. A stronger force has prevailed in Colindale and further diluted this north London facsimile of the suburban dream, where tree-lined streets are in short supply. The houses look empty as if that's telling something about what goes on indoors. Front gardens are trumped by an overwhelming need for off-street parking, and the cars look in better shape than the houses. Sightlines are uninterrupted by landscaping, privacy and sound absorption are wrecked. Only an occasional people-mover acts as a barrier. The streets look bald and weary, as though a crop has failed. The walk from the tube is dispiriting and familiar: out-of-town retail warehouses and HQs for high-street midgets; uneven pavements fronting no-hope enterprises; and plenty of cut-price shops selling useful cheap plastic items. It's a high street too rundown even for charity shops, a vista that must point to the end of something.

Going to Colindale isn't about sightseeing, that's for sure. She'll show you the sites instead: here is where it happened, or so she's been told. She's going after the clues she's planted. Following leads that she's chased in herself. Anyone might wonder who's exposing what about whom here. She's going to see what traces of Ant remain, what the site of his private existence can tell her. That's what she said. It's taken 40 years but she knows now that there are two *n*s in Ennerdale even though she hasn't written it on the front of an envelope of a christmas card or birthday thank you for such a long time. She can imagine the house into existence through the memory of an address written down in a small, unnecessary book. That's what she remembers more clearly than the house itself, words on paper rather than the building.

Shielded by a row of houses from the high street, the section of the A5 known as The Hyde, Ennerdale Drive runs to the top of a hill and forms the central spine of an inverted U-shape. The layout creates an almost self-contained neighborhood, like a village, as the refrain from estate agents and vendors goes. The street itself is narrow, the few cars parked are mostly half up on the pavement. Here too in almost every house, but not the one that she still thinks of as her uncle's, the owner has concreted over the once-prized front garden to provide in lieu the contemporary trophy of private parking space. It makes for a barren but broader space, and the driveways mean there's less need to contest the public territory of the street. No one was worrying much about the effects on the watertable or the more visible boundaries of defensible space that foliage provides. For a once-leafy suburb the tree count is decidedly and noticeably thin in this season of blossom. Two or three small circular islands with low-maintenance planting sit in the length of the road, greening it up a touch, slowing down what little traffic there is, reducing density by splitting the line of houses.

● ● ●

So I'm looking for remembrance still. The darkness of the entrance, the arched portico and glass-paned door, the privet-edged path, all seeming so familiar, beckon me in, with something other than a welcome. I can pretend that I'm recognizing 2 Ennerdale Drive over the many other houses like it whose front paths I have walked up in other north London suburbs built by developers in the early twentieth century. Like memorists of antiquity I use the hedge and porch as prompts for where I am in the story, to substitute place as memory. The hall light is off and the curtains are drawn, even though it's hardly dark yet. I knock with the letterplate handle. Long pause.

I say beckon me in, but it doesn't. The house is set up for the opposite effect. It's semi-detached, for a start. I'm just ignoring the warning signs. Not everybody needs to have a dog. It's not like I really remember any of this but something's being mapped out. There's no getting away with dawdling up that garden path. It's straight up and down, single file and don't touch the hedge. Intruders are repelled by layout alone. That sneaky glazed portico deliberately gives the wrong impression: there's no transparency like the false promise of see-through glass, no transparency at all. It's obscurity, and one-way at that. No need for fortifications, with a frontage like this; the whole place is a characterization of them.

It isn't only the house. Much is communicated by the streetscape, the layout of exterior space, the front doors positioned as far from each other as possible, the gates and defined paths. I was wrong. These houses don't look empty so much as unlived-in, a silence of neatness that deters visitors and keeps chancers at bay by making sure they are fully informed of the state of its insides: the exterior a reflection of the great unused indoors. The house is a physical manifestation of a dream, the dream-house of the individual, in Walter Benjamin's terms; this one is without possibility but not short on ambiguity.

Inside and out, it's all façade. Nobody's feeling at home here. An inconsiderable frontage in itself but that's the whole of it. Somewhere a big cork stopper interrupts the tidal flow of lived existence, chamber upon chamber of cellar space, itself constituting an archive of life unlived, an existence disbarred from living. The exterior is, or at least appears to be, always knowable; the interior is more mysterious, accessible only partially and then by invitation.

I'm thinking that I shouldn't have come, that I should have come ten years ago, that I should have come at any time during the last 20 years, but not now. What am I here for, what do I expect? The pause gets longer and I bang the handle again sharply. I try to look through the spy mirror even though I know it's only there to look back at me, not the other way about. It's not for monitoring indoors, it's for keeping account of who's trying to get in from the outside. This is a life that is defined above all else by the distinction between interior and exterior: policing the boundary at all times, whatever the cost.

Without warning of footsteps or lights coming on, the door is opened a little, so I'm surprised and say nothing. There's silence and a wave of interior pours out. She peers at me, as though groggy. She doesn't know who I am. Advantage me, but it doesn't feel like one. All I want is – well, what? To come inside and what then? As if I want to be ushered into the front parlor as the prodigal great-niece and send out for a Fuller's walnut cake.

Any second she'll go 'Yes?' or 'Not today, thank you.' I can't see inside but I can tell she's very, and strangely, well dressed. I half expect her to be wearing hat and gloves. I haven't interrupted the spring-cleaning then. Then again, she could be doing just that, the suburban lady making light of her work. A knock at this door is never going to be anything other than an interruption. There is no mat on my side of the front door and it would not say welcome. Instead a metal grille sits in front of the step to stop cattle or anything else crossing the threshold.

She's opened the door a crack more, enough to let me sidle in, no grand gestures here. It's a privilege nonetheless, the front door must be heavily guarded to secure the space between danger and safety. I give her my card so she can see the name in print but she's still not having it and peers at it as if to detect forgery. I'm not who I say I am. I almost say 'Don't you know who I am?' but I can tell she's not going to fall for that. And who am I to her, after all? There's no connection, whichever way you look at it: wrong side of the family, wrong generation, wrong decade, wrong gender too I expect. The lot.

A house of small, disconnected containments, we stand just inside the hall, breathless in the airlock, keeping me separate from her privacy in this antechamber, closer than either of us would like to be. She bars my way to penetration further into the house without doing a thing. I'm not going to get as far as the sitting room, that's a privacy too far. The hall will have to tell me all I need to know, as it does for most of the visitors. She's already told me that he's out. Now she says, 'We're having our evening meal,' but I can't smell anything except dank furnishings and she's not going to tell me who's joining her for dinner. Her imaginary friend Johnny Walker, I'd say. I'm lucky she's not going to invite me to join them.

In the corner, by the very closed door of the front sitting room, is a small telephone table, its appliance resting on a bleak square of threadwork that must have been made under better lighting than this. The parlor is at once a space of refined but firm containment and also a certain expansiveness, the public space of the private sphere. The coverings of plush and half-cut moquette might act as swaddling but attach the shape and physical detritus, the dust and sweat and hair, of habits and poses. I don't have to see it to know.

The kitchen door at the end of the corridor is paneled in glass and shielded from any inquiries by its pattern. The life of the house needs protection from more than my gaze. Everything is so protected it's entirely exposed: the hall runner by a plastic overlay, covered in turn by a doorway mat; secrets screened by the dim yellow light. A collection of footprints and paths through the house reveal far more stories than those they sheath and protect from the damage of exposure, but never giving anything away. Flooring and upholstery, themselves coverings, are preserved as secondary defenses for further layers of the stories planted by the tread of inhabitants and any triumphant interlopers. All this settles into another layer to muffle, deflect and absorb the sound and shock of everyday life. The prize of suburbia is that it brings a highly distinctive lack of disturbance of noise or everyday violence or the perceived dangers of proximity to the masses.

From the street side the front door, while guarded in a recess beneath its arched porch, is wreathed in light and glass. Some effort has gone into mitigating this effect indoors. The runner continues up the staircase, but no plastic sheathing is needed there apparently. It's like a b&b where access to bedrooms is a policing matter. I turn around the long way as I leave, to get a glimpse of what I hadn't been able to see before. This is as far as your road goes. Set by the phone, pencil inserted in its holder, is a dial-up address book, ancient but pristine, where numbers for other Mrs As are inscribed. The telephone brings invaders no more welcome than me. The same wallpaper is hung up the stairway, its floral pattern as pretty as the neighborhood they, the suburban dwellers, imagined they would live in, now all faded, colors and warmth long gone. I can't see any more than this, there's no delaying. Whatever I want, I'm not going to be welcome. She won't risk me telling any tales. I'm looking, looking in, that's insult enough to merit closed doors. With a goodbye so polite it blisters, I'm out again to be guided down the privet strait to take me safely off the premises. I breathe. Inside, there's no reason to stop holding on.

• • •

No.2

When she went to look at 2 Ennerdale Drive, one year after it had been sold and two years after Ant's death, she thought irrationally that the new owners had been slow to make it their own. It's true there were no visible external signs of new occupancy since the last owner, apart from the satellite dish and she's still making assumptions that it wasn't Ant's. Some of the old metal window frames, specified because they don't rot like wooden ones, are still thick with layers of paint. She can see that from the pavement. Few examples of the originals remain in the street, they are mostly now snug-fitting uPVC replacements and some of the new porches and windows have plastic approxima-tions of the stained-glass panes from designs of housing a few decades later than these in the top-hinged segments of the casement windows. The shrouded ground-floor windows at the front of the house are not original. As replacements go, they are not recent. Now they are faux leaded lights but she can't see whether the 'leads' are in fact taped segments on a single pane.

The untamed privet hedge at no.2 sways in the spring breeze. Occupying a pane of door glass is a politely worded but menacing itemized list of a keep out notice. The curious italics, especially the open shape of his *es*, more like *ms* sat on their sides, are immediately recognizable as Ant's. The wonder is how long the notice has lasted. The print is faded, moisture has caused the lettering to bleed into a fuzzy mass but that could happen over a single season through condensation and sunlight. The current deliverers of the message have seen fit to continue this ancient broadcast, not bothering to replace it with an updated version in their own hand or from their own printer. The notice is stuck on to one of the panes in the upper half of the door just above the letterbox that is not to receive free newspapers, sales leaflets or circulars nor to deliver any offence nor to heed the knocks on it from any callers other than those of the postman and representatives of the essential services to whom many thanks. It's a well-crafted item, even droll in its way with 'no offence intended' listed as an entry. Each item on the list is lined up beneath each other, all neatly centered. He's restricting access to the invited and the expected and the essential: it's a guest list for his private performance at home. But in trying not to give offence he's reaching for the impossible because these notices always come from the pen of Mr Angry of Curmudgeon Street. It's asking for it: dogshit, fireworks, knocking at all hours. It could be described as a form of territorial paranoid even, a deposit of the suburban separation shilling. It makes a blot on the perfect entity of a front door and yet the true nature of the house sings out through every word of it. Privacy is at a premium, built-in.

In a full-frontal view, that overlooking window panel of next door's bow is peeking into the frame: oh no you don't, I'm here too you know, don't think you can forget me. This intrusion, this shameless waving at the camera, also indicates how the design of the house works. The ambiguities inherent in the semi-detached suburban are immediately apparent. There's no place for the dividing line between the semis to sit happily. The house is desperate to be singular, individual, as they all are, yet it's the same as the one next door, only transposed. It's attached, semi, but making an effort to pretend to be detached by placing its front door as far away from the other house as the building can stand. A side section of its bow window, on both ground and first floors, faces the same window next door. It's always there.

Suburban life's characteristic clarity of distinction between public and private life insists on a distinct lack of ambiguity regarding the separation of spheres. It works in intention, if not in execution. New arrangements of streets and buildings requested lives to aspire to, suggested guidelines for the roles to be played in them. Daily life in this house is organized precisely to maintain and shore up distinctions of interior and exterior existence, within and without the walls, to keep any seepage or intermingling of the two to a minimum.

The impression and the house itself, then, can never be quite satisfactory. It's impossible to see the whole house without seeing the other, the let's-pretend-it's-not-there, the same but completely alien, house. The house is never quite finished as a structure, it can only ever be a half. Never finished as a home either, anyone would think. To place the bow window on the outer edge of the design, allowing a wider purview and a better chance of looking away beyond that other attachment, ignoring it or willfully not seeing it, looking instead at the wider world, has an equally unacceptable effect. The front doors would then have to be next to each other. They would be closer than might be comfortable, leading to the specter of meetings on the garden paths. Worse still, from a distance, perspective might overlap the two into a single, shared route.

Bisecting the chimneystack that serves both houses is another possibility for division. It would leave ragged bricks and edges but that's as nothing compared with looking at the roof, a single expanse of neat, tessellated pattern. Tiny units fixed together make a whole. It looks wrong, to be unable to see the totality; just a plain regular red-tiled hipped roof but it's still a cruel cut to avoid seeing the whole. Desperation for even an illusion of the grandeur of a larger house (and in bird's eye view only) increases the value of this single benefit.

There's no way then to see this building or even to take a photograph of this house, half or whole, entire or split, one way or the other. The bow window pushes outward, the front door is set into the porch. It stands back, thrown into garlanded relief by the carved arch. It recedes. Don't look outwards and don't come in either. Photography renders the 12 glass panes of the front door, and the four on either side of the doorframe, black and impenetrable. That could be as much as there is to say, only it's irresistible to point out that the glass, except for the one pane covered with the 'no circulars' sign, has a lightly rippled textured surface, allowing light into the house and only a skewed, diminished view into the hall. Only insiders can know what's going on; inside behind the semi-opaque glass and behind the shielding net curtains.

Unlike a (more modern) house where design can be used to complicate and extend the ideas of interior and exterior, 2 Ennerdale Drive carves a sharp distinction between the two. The whole notion of this house exists to express the distinctions of inside/outside; home/away; us/them. It cleaves to a spatial model that demands a series of illusory, unequivocal separations, where everything and everyone has their place and everyone knows it. Any uncertainty or blurring about what belongs where is precisely what the suburbs were designed to stop. That's their purpose. Yet the ambiguity of its staple, the semi-detached house, is plain for all to see.

The curtains are also part of the security measures, protecting the interior. Bulbous hedges screen the front garden, reaching to a height that screens off the bottom third of the window and the inner edge of the front door with its small letterbox and no bell. The quick-march garden path is flanked by knee-high hedging on both sides, a privet guard of honor. Deep glossy green hedging complements the overwhelming redness of the building: red brick, red roof, red-blocked steps and path, red hanging tiles. Harsh white details of the pointing, the guttering and downpipes, the windowframes and the front door make the red redder and the green even brighter. It should stand out, which can't have been the desired effect, but it doesn't. It's drab, not quiet. The curved edges of the privet look out of place with the angularity of the house, it makes a jarring contrast of sharpness and flat planes apart from the brickwork arch. It's all very neat, the endless rectangles of bricks and tiles and window panes only interrupted by the satellite dish and entirely alien and protruding pieces of water pipe spoiling the lines. It's an ugly house.

Ant spent his whole life, more or less, living in no.2 in Colindale, in the middle of all this prescription and ambiguity. Born eight years after the house was completed, it was the place he always returned to. She had been wanting to talk to him. She wanted to store up material from a small pool of fast-diminishing resources, for when she finally got a feel to write a book about the impossibility of family narrative. She wanted to hear Ant's stories about Richard and Henry, and about their careers and his. She wanted details from one who knew. She wanted some facts at least, and ones that she would not find in a book. Privileged facts they would be and so very probably facts not at all but ones she could choose to believe in. Separations between home and outside, between public and private lives were more sharply and differently demarcated at that time, the semi-detached spacious suburbs reinscribing this over again, and the divisions between the guarded privacy of home and the life outside were probably even more distinct for an actor.

To get beyond the biography and anecdotes, to uncover the secrets and lies, would be a huge bonus she hardly dared hope for. Even professional actors fall under the spell of the recording machine, forfeiting their privacy in the intimacy of the interview, forgetting the link between conversation and the printed word. Carefully choreographed 'slips' have long been a contract between entertainment and the PR side of media, whether for infotainment, making it up or laying false trails. It's the price paid, and is rewarded handsomely enough as a source. Actors vivify other people on stage, their work isn't about bringing their own existence to life. Ant might genuinely have had nothing to tell her. Or nothing that she would want to know. What if she could ask Ant the questions? What if she knew what they were? And if he wanted to tell her, what if he knew the answers? What if he told her?

She'd written to him maybe ten years before his death. He'd replied, winningly, with a note in his strange italic handwriting and didn't promise much. So, pausing only for a couple of years to gather her nerve again, she called him. He was less charming on the phone. Maybe he didn't relish being interviewed by a member of his own family. Maybe he realized sooner than she did how mixed were her motives. His voice conveyed little of the warmth of feeling that she'd somewhat disingenuously imagined she could rely upon. And Ant, as she learned appropriately enough in his obituary, was an intensely private man.

He made it clear that he didn't think he had much to say on the subject of acting and family, that he wasn't too keen on the idea of talking about it on tape. Then: 'I haven't had a drink for 27 years and three months. Do you drink?' He sounded even less keen when she said yes. He was about to go on tour; he'd call her when he'd got back and take her for lunch. Bereft of options she pretended to herself that it would happen, that it was dependent on her contacting him to organize it. She kept saying that she must do it before he died but she didn't and then he did.

She wanted to use him to plug gaps, to gather a little more substance to chew over. She wanted to plunder his archive, to mine it quite heartlessly for stuffing to bulk up the paltry pickings of her memory. It was as though the addition of someone else's probably highly, but differently, selective assortment of family stories and theatrical anecdotes would strengthen the thin tissues of her own; as though his archival holdings would somehow validate her poor showing. He would help her achieve the critical mass required to make some kind of semi-authoritative account in whatever it was she was going to do with this information. If, as Roland Barthes has it, you can only recognize someone through fragments, she thought hearing those belonging to someone else's memory would help. Since she didn't know what they were, she couldn't know what she was looking for or what to ask or what the questions would have been, had she had a chance to ask them.

The myth of the coherent identity-tale, that imagined wholeness, is very potent. It's pervasive and pernicious and she strives to buy into it constantly, with longing, as she writes her way out of it, gasping for uncertainty. It's something like the lingering desire for a happy ending, or at least a resolution. She'd have to dismiss it for being too neat. She'd need to make it up and then buy into it in a way that nothing in the world has ever encouraged her to do. With satisfaction would come the end of the story, but not vice versa. So lack and missing remain the only way to carry on, the only tale in town.

There's no one to sit her down and supply all the answers, the authorized version, in a seamlessly molded story where everyone knows their place and sticks to the script. Such roles are fulfilled in public, on stage. A shared script doesn't necessarily exist in private life on the domestic stage. It's all improvised instead. This is a modern production: there's a sense of loss, of absence. It's set mostly in the twentieth century after all. It could be that the missing is the characters' limited appearances onstage, in real time anyway. Still, there's no shortage of plans or of stories made of maps and buildings to follow. And if such a person existed to spin her that yarn, she wouldn't buy it. If Ant had agreed to a lengthy series of interviews and had turned out to be a forthcoming and expansive interviewee, there still would never have been a complete, bounded picture and finished work because how should it, would it, finish? She would pick at it and unravel little bits, fray a hem here and there, for a little mystery. Face value? She wouldn't have it if you were giving it away.

• • •

Laing's company stamp on the area prevails. In 2006 traffic signs and street lamps along the route from Colindale tube station to Ennerdale Drive have Polyboard signs for a Laing's development taped to their shanks, pointing in the direction of Edgware and Brent Cross. Laing's hasn't stood still either. The signs might be pointing the way to the last housing development Laing's ever built. The house that Laing's built in Ennerdale Drive is up for sale, and so is the company.

The longevity of John Laing & Co suggests a company that has excelled at its work. The company restructured in 2001 following a hostile takeover bid for the property company in 1982, and this involved divesting itself of all house-building and property interests in favor of infrastructure projects through government funding initiatives. In leaving behind their traditional profile Laing's have ditched their company history: on their website, the 'history' section stretches only back to 2001, although mention is made of James Laing, grandfather of John. James Laing founded the company in 1848, as a local builder in a village near Carlisle.

Their considerable heritage in British industry and lengthy reputation clearly marks them out as reliable candidates for partnership roles in long-term projects with central and local government. These initiatives can have a duration of 25 to 30 years, so Laing's is involved in shaping policies, cannily tapping into lucrative currents and defining the array of options available to the public, presented as choices. Public and private is the trick and Laing's doesn't miss it.

Working on contracts to improve and replace public buildings and infrastructure such as unsafe schools, unsanitary and unfit-for-purpose hospitals, dripping and hazardous Victorian water and drainage systems is made considerably less risky than, say, speculative house building. Currently, they're working on something a little different. Laing's is still supplying accommo-dation for growing populations. These days the company is engaged in contracts for prisons; in the 1920s the housing was for families wanting to light out for the suburbs. One population was to be kept away from general society and another was keen to keep themselves apart. The system of staggered payments in such projects represents a long-term and stable return. Contractual arrangements are also less fraught with the financial, architectural and physical risks of construction because the burdens are borne largely by others, the taxpayers and the contractors. Legislation is used to make public building contracts more attractive (more lucrative) to private companies. Laing's has been managing 48 of these Public Finance Initiative projects worth £335 million.

Her interest doesn't stretch to tracking the growth of Laing's many incarnations and subsidiaries. By chance she reads an obituary for Maurice Laing 'industrialist and benefactor', the second son of John, who from unpromising beginnings as 'a sickly child with a speech impediment' (*The Guardian*, 25 February 2008) went on to become the first head of the Confederation of British Industry. She notices the takeover story too and reads that some of the original shareholders would be getting a windfall of 138p a share in cash. The bid of £886.9

million worth 355p per share came from the Henderson Group in September 2006, and was followed by a hike in share prices to 360p. Allianz then topped the offer with 385p before Henderson came back again. For a while Laing's is added to a short list of words that she scans the financial pages for. And then, two months after the original bid, Allianz, the rival bidder, pulls out and the directors of Laing recommend the Henderson terms. Shares in Laing fall to 402p, 'reflecting disappointment that the Germans refused to raise their terms.' In less time than it takes to sell a semi-detached, it's over.

Chapter 2

Private lives

2 Ennerdale Drive is an ordinary, mid-size semi, built by John Laing and Co in 1926 and inhabited by members of the same family from then until 2005. A blink of an eye, you might say, or a lifetime span. To a disconnected and fairly rootless family, a life spent in the same country or even continent has been unusual and relocating seemed to be the norm, for reasons of poverty, love, escape or politics. In a family for whom discontinuity is the pattern, the existence of 2 Ennerdale Drive could cast a net of reassurance across the narrative.

The house doesn't tell her the whole story; it's the steam on the surface, the dust round the edges, the set for the first act only. From when it was first inhabited, 2 Ennerdale Drive was both somewhere to stay put and go forth from, for aunties and brothers. The detective can follow their lead, go further afield and keep checking back home.

The family bought the house new and it passed through three generations of unmarried ownership, from great-aunt to mother to son. It was Ant and Fred's two great-aunts, who came to be women of property in a district that was springing up in north London. Whether the great-aunts remained single through choice or through circumstance is unknown. Excluded by sheer lack of men of marriageable age if not inclination from the narrative of marriage, a generation of women was consigned to the quiet life by the scale of deaths in the Great War and the Flu Epidemic that followed it. That's not the whole story, thankfully. And it's not the story for these two either.

Their resources allowed Great-Aunt Ennerdale to fund both the purchase of a new, though relatively modest, family home and a desire to travel and see some of what was left of Europe and beyond after the war. These aunties were in a highly enviable position compared to women facing dull lives on the edges of families not quite theirs with scant possibility for meaningful or financially worthwhile employment or training. Colindale didn't 'spring up' in a spontaneous or springtime eruption of early suburb, it was squeezed into existence through a coincidence of temporal and spatial circumstances and responses – war, pollution, snobbery, legislation, class hatred, desire, business, innovation and tradition, reaction and technology. Some of this is clear and acknowledged; some of it is unmissable; some of it unmentionable.

The great-aunts amply fill the roles of two familiar if fading characters of their time. One was an intrepid globe-trotter, primed to go forth and then return to a quieter life in the suburbs where her sister kept house for her as a bolthole to return to between trips. They play the two-fold parts of the storyteller in Walter Benjamin's dichotomy; one tells the story of home and the other of elsewhere and this division too they share with their grand-nephews who also inhabited a role each as traveler and home-dweller. A life shared, and apart, it didn't stand still. They passed the house on to their niece, mother of Fred and Antony. By the time the house passed to their generation, one grand-nephew had already made his home in Seattle. The other stayed home with his mum, and followed family traditions.

As a location to begin raveling strands of family narrative, even this 'godforsaken part of Hendon near the M1' as one guidebook has it, becomes interesting. Sited on or near the old hamlet of Colindeep, the unlikely named Colindale is an unfash-ionable suburb to the north-west of London, way beyond the radiance of the smart lights of Hampstead. In their manifestation as urban fringe-overspill, it may be hard now to credit how Colindale and other local suburbs that were cultivated into existence at the same time could have been imagined to even partially fulfill its promise. These districts may have themselves become cluttered, over-developed outer London drive-throughs lacking cohesion. But Colindale has its attractions. It wasn't only the possibility for social advancement to which hopeful suburbanites responded. Some attractions cannot be overstated: broad, uncrowded avenues and uncongested public space, a feeling of spaciousness in private homes as well as a less polluted, more leafy existence and previously unheard-of facilities, close by new sites of employment or close to the means of transport to get to work in town. Contemporary figures continue to underline the importance of accepting the draw of the suburbs: a report published by the Joseph Rowntree Foundation in 2005 suggested that 86 per cent of the UK population live in suburbs.

The influence of John Laing & Co in the area began when the company purchased 30 acres of land in Colindale in the early 1920s for £750 per acre. By 1925 they had bought land and built in Eltham, Esher, Woolwich and Mill Hill too, where the company's first national headquarters were sited and where the eponymous head of the company also built his own home on his move south from Carlisle. Business was clearly good. In 1928 the flotation of Laing Properties was announced, a vehicle for the company's new property holdings, under whose aegis the Colindale development came. These preferential shares were intended to encourage younger members of staff to invest financially and emotionally in the new company, without alienating earlier shareholders by diminishing their income from the original issue. It was transparent and it worked.

Colindale's house-building boom was generated in part by the need to accommodate the workforce of the nearby aviation factories. In 1909 a local company, Everett & Edgcombe, had built a plane and started the process of turning the place into Aero City, if not the 'Charing Cross of our international air routes' envisaged by local aviation entrepreneur Claude Grahame-White. Two years later Grahame-White bought their airfield and hangar and promoted it as the London Aerodrome. Although aircraft production during the First World War hastened its growth, the area that was to carry the name of Colindale remained largely rural until the 1920s when an agglomeration of several factors contributed to major changes in land-use from hamlet to suburb. Grahame-White's company built Aeroville close by the aerodrome to house 300 employees in an echo of Bournville, the village built near Birmingham in the late nineteenth century to house workers at Cadbury's chocolate factory. Aeroville's first resident arrived in 1919 and it still luxuriates in the glory of that one-word address. It is a two-storey square of simple terraced flats, designed by Henry Matthews. Grahame-White continued to develop the recreational potential of the aerodrome before moving on to car and furniture manufacturing. His legacy lingers in the naming of the Grahame Park district and a Grahame-White House in Queensbury. It was this long history of aviation that led to the RAF Museum moving to the area in 1972.

Interwar growth in manufacturing industries further accelerated development of the area. Food processing, furniture and electrical equipment industries spread from Burnt Oak all along The Hyde, Colindale's main road, and down into Cricklewood. By the Second World War manufacturing premises for ball bearings, tennis racquets, speedometers, potato peelers and hair curlers were sited there too. Franco Illuminated signs, famed manufacturer of neon signs installed in Piccadilly until the 1970s, came to nearby Aerodrome Road in 1922. Factory employees had to be housed locally or encouraged to use the newly extended transport network to travel from inner London to work. Increased opportunities for secure employment allowed an expansion of the mortgage-holding classes among middle-class people and its extension for the first time to a significant minority of working-class households. Government subsidy and loosening of mortgage requirements were also put into place to extend private property ownership. Wages for work considered the province of working-class or lower-middle-class people ranged widely from 30/- (30 shillings; 20 shillings made up one pound in pre-decimal currency) to £9.00. According to Laing's biography the most common livelihoods among buyers of their spec houses were mechanics, clerks and laborers.

Both builders and building societies were keen to claim credit for providing improved and affordable homes for working-class people to buy. Building societies were enabled to advance 90 per cent of the purchase price on a loan over 20 or 25 years. Mortgage repayments on lower-end speculatively built (spec) houses could be as low or less than rents. A £50 deposit could secure a small three-bed semi-detached home costing £595. With mortgages of not much more than £1 per week for a standard semi, and the difference in monthly repayments between the cheapest and most expensive designs at 3s/3d (three shillings and three pence; or about 17p in a straight exchange from £sd to decimal currency), purchasers could buy a defined space, their territory. They bought the security of the sense of their own place.

Growth in manufacturing, and the burgeoning aircraft industry in particular may have been pivotal in indicating sites for residential development in the area, but the extension of railway and underground train lines were major ingredients fostering suburban development. The Northern Line reached Edgware, including a stop at Colindale, in the 1920s and by 1924 rush hour trains ran about every eight minutes from Edgware to Moorgate and every four minutes from Golders Green to Charing Cross. As soon as there was a station to stop at, the London Underground group began promoting the 'little palaces' of newly built suburban homes that were now within reach, forging the chain of mutual gratitude between developer and transport authorities. Colindale station was a grand affair at that time, fronted by a wide portico projecting out the full width of the pavement and supported by four pairs of columns.

Roadbuilding powered development of the suburbs too, and car ownership increased enormously in the same period. Work began on the innovatory North Circular Road in 1924, the northern hemisphere of London's orbital roadway. It runs about a mile from Ennerdale Drive and about twice that distance from the Newspaper Library, now known as the British Library Newspaper Reading Room. A horse and cart was still carrying the weekly deliveries of newspapers between Colindale and the British Library in Bloomsbury only seven years before the house in Ennerdale Drive was built. A copy of every newspaper published in English (and many in other languages) is held there, either in the original paper version or on microfilm. In 1940 a Luftwaffe bomb destroyed the building erected in place of the original Newspaper Repository sited in Colindale since 1903, and an estimated 6000 volumes of newspapers were destroyed and a further 15,00 volumes damaged. In 2007 writers, historians and people interested in knowing more about their family tree make pilgrimage to Colindale to one of the world's oldest and largest newspaper libraries, where a product designed to be short-lived, read and discarded, is protected for prosperity.

The North Circular Road was superseded only in the late 1980s by the outer circle route of the M25, a pet project of Margaret Thatcher, with her legendary disdain for public transport and its users. The capacity of the M25 was insufficient even before it was opened.

The growth of suburbs like Colindale in the 1920s also consti-tuted a local response to a national housing shortage, and in 1924 an Act passed by Ramsey MacDonald's Labour government launched a 15-year building program of 2.5 million houses. (To compare the scale of the crisis and the ambition of the response, in the ten years from 1997 with housing shortages again at critical levels, around 1.6 million newbuild houses were started.) John Betjeman, the bard of the west London suburbs (Metropolitan rather than Northern Line) described Kingsbury as where 'a speculative builder ... let himself go, in the Twenties.' And clearly they were able to let themselves go fast. Three million new homes were built for sale in the 1920s and 1930s. Very little local authority town planning control was enforced. Apart from drainage, which had crucial implications for a sense of cultural aspiration as well as being essential infrastructure, and road width standards, builders were allowed to get on with the job untrammeled. It was not until 1945 that the town planning system was established, in part as a means to regulate the growth of the suburbs.

Exhibit 2: Live at Edgware and Live!

London Underground invites you to 'Live at Edgware and live!' with this poster designed to look like a sampler, a piece of embroidery fabricated to display the producer's skills and knowledge of a variety of stitches.

The artist Helen Brice was one of a number of prominent interwar commercial artists commissioned to design posters for a series extolling the delights of the suburban life and the countryside brought within easy reach by the extension of the tube line. She created a compact tale, within a stylized border of foliage (red-hot pokers, popular suburban flowers that originate in Africa), with an economic use of block color in turquoise, orange and pale yellow and a strong use of symbol. She uses a squared-off style on both lettering and images, suggestive of blanket stitch, making more brickiness of it than embroidery needs to do when painting pictures with stitches. The lettering is drawn to look uneven, with strokes of different weight. The clothes Brice's characters wear are drawn in similar styles, their empire-line dresses and frock coats suggestive of the eighteenth century.

This design uses a tongue-in-cheek approach to underline the weight of its invocation; the appeal of this pill has no need to be heavily sugared. It's an easy read, even with its archaic language and use of

capital letters. The story goes like this: an Englishman's home should be a castle but often he is forced to make do with a cramped house in a polluted, crowded city. The improved environment in Edgware where his very much larger and grander detached residence is located means that he can dispense with his handkerchief, stop sneezing over the dog and no longer has any need of his umbrella. The house is flanked by trees and gates and is larger than anything else on the page, larger than a whole terrace of town houses, larger than a railway carriage, larger than a fantasy castle. The new house in Edgware is a set on which the new family life can play out, where the sun always shines and life is healthy. The train carriages in which he travels to the city to work are properly named Enterprise, Triumph and Venture, an accurate description of his life in Edgware for his family has now grown to include livestock, bees and fowl as well as six children, two servants and a cat to add to the wife and dog already in place at the top of the page.

There dwelt a Man in the City of London, but the Fogs and Smoke thereof did cause him such ill-ease, that he said unto his Wife, My Love, Let us adventure unto Edgware & there buy us an House out of Income. Thus did they acquire an House of rare Beauty & commodious withal. The Man did journey daily unto the City, retuning with joy into the clear country Air. In the Garden they planted Fruit-trees, the which, flourishing mightily, did bring them no small gain, so that presently they were able to purchase also – a Cock, A Hen a Cow, some Bees, a Horse, a Duck & a Drake. In this way they did fare sumptuously and prosper beyond all expectation.

'Saying in their Gladness,' the punchline goes, 'Truly, Good Fortune does travel by Underground'.

Samplers often incorporate numbers, motifs, alphabets and verses and are made to mark weddings and births and anniversaries. They offer homely pieces of stitched moral guidance, lest we forget. Samplers are one-offs, unlike the house and this poster, which is a mass-produced representation designed to look like a handmade piece of domestic craftwork. As if it were a real sampler, Helen Brice has included her name as the 'embroiderer' and the date, 1924. At the bottom left-hand edge of the poster, large enough to be visible even on a scaled-down print, is the printer credit to Vincent Books Day & Son Ltd, Lith (lithographic printers) London WC2, where the London Transport Museum who supplied the print is now located. At the right-hand edge are the numbers 1000 817 5.6.25: print run, number in run and date of printing.

The word sampler comes from the Latin exemplum, 'an example to be followed', whether as a model demonstrating numeracy and literacy or as simple pattern. More usually though, a sampler shows a motto, a message like 'Home Sweet Home' or 'Welcome', which would be selected for the space in which it would eventually appear, often hanging over doors or in halls.

Many of the transport posters from this period and through the 1930s depict a standard domestic scene of women caring for children and doing housework or welcoming their husbands home after their journey on the good train Enterprise. This operates both as an encouragement to others to move out to the suburban life, where gender roles are considered to be anchored to the traditional forms and perhaps also as a tonic to those who are aware that such a move has, for many, meant more women returning to or staying in the workplace. Amid the uncertainties of the interwar years, a woman's role could still be represented as something to be relied upon, especially if in reality it couldn't anymore.

Frank Pick, who was head of London Underground in the 1910s and 1920s, began commissioning posters from 1908 and also commissioned the London Transport roundel, which came into use in the same year. Pick lived near Golders Green so would have benefitted himself from the extension of the Northern Line. Clearly a man who understood the importance of strong design, he was the force behind the station map, station design and upholstery by artists such as Man Ray and Paul Nash. For their graphics, London Underground used the New Johnston typeface designed in 1916 by Edward Johnston, which was thought to embody the ideals of suburban life. Transport for London, the company now running London's transport systems, still owns the copyright. The widely used Gill Sans is a reworking of it and a Truetype approximation of New Johnston exists called Paddington, presumably after the railway station.

The architect largely responsible for the modern style and the innovative use of exposed concrete in the new stations, such as the curved cylindrical forms on the Piccadilly line, was Charles Holden. His station designs, inspired by work in Scandinavia, Germany and the Netherlands, reflected the spirit of the International Style and were made possible through the use of new technologies. At the same time, the designers of most of the housing to which the trains delivered their passengers, that the trains made it possible to live in, dismissed and ignored them.

In 1927 Michael Hendy designed a poster titled 'The next move (and take a season ticket)' caricaturing a family in the crazed throes of house removal, stressed but on their way to a street of detached houses. 'Come in to play, Come out to live: Buy a season ticket' was the advice on a 1936 poster by the renowned First World War artist Paul Nash, encouraging employees to stay in town after work or to 'come in' at weekends, to enjoy and swell the city's riches during their time off work. Late-night opening for shops and galleries and cheap off-peak tickets were introduced in the interwar years and brought women with leisure time into town for shopping and sightseeing. The 'horrors' of nighttime urban pleasure are rendered harmless by the ability to escape to the safety of the suburbs. A companion piece, 'Come out to play' in the countryside surrounding London reminded those people unable or unwilling to move out that the rural delights could be extended to them even if only temporarily for the price of an underground ticket. Charles Paine's poster design in 1929 uses a pair of blackbirds reduced to living in the guttering of a town house, blossoming into full-blown nest-building in leafy suburbia at the bottom of the illustration with the slogan 'A change of residence is as good as a holiday'. Whichever your direction and whatever your goal, travel by London Underground was part of the answer. Each one highly individual, the posters echo and stoke the excitement of moving out of town or of being within easy reach of town and (almost) country.

To imagine the interiors of houses like 2 Ennerdale Drives is to place the woman of the house immediately and unusually center stage of her own domestic sphere. In the living room and dining room (if the budget runs to that), the traditional family-life tableau is firmly in place.

See Father! See Father tend the garden! See Father read the paper! See Father survey the family from his armchair! See Father rush to the underground with his briefcase! See Father smoke his pipe in the sitting room when he returns from work! See Father build the edifice of his family, separate from all the others. See Father play Father!

See Mummy in the kitchen! See Mummy bask in the glow of family life! See Mummy cook and clean! See Mummy work at it! See Mummy make it look easy! Watch Mummy serve the dinner! See Mummy play the game! See Mummy!

She started to call him 'Father' when the children came, and somehow it sticks. It's more than a name and he says he's not even sure that he doesn't like it, being father of the family. She thinks to herself that he's more of a stranger to her now than he has been since they were married, with his travelling back and forward into town all week although it's only 40 minutes to the office. There's no time in the morning as she's getting the household up and breakfasted and then he's off to the station to take his place in the tide of all the other husbands to be whisked up to town. He exchanges a nod with one or two. He likes to keep to himself.

Now the children stay up a little later and there is a short time before she's getting their tea ready, when they are gathered together in the same room. He has a look at the paper, the children play quietly or look at a picture book. Sometimes, if he's not too tired, he might tell them a funny story about the office, and often there's a look or a wink to let her know that he has more of the story to tell her later after the children have gone up. The fire will be going and he'll catch her glance that she's thinking even now of her relief when they came to the new house and she saw that she wasn't going to be cleaning out a dirty grate every day. They sometimes all fall asleep, her and the children, that is. If she nods off in her chair, the children are fascinated and quieter than they ever are, as if they can't quite believe that their mummy sleeps at all. He watches. He likes to look at them. We're all together, happy here, he's sure of that. Not so long ago they had company, right here in this room, people from across the way but even that cannot please her like this scene does. And that is how he likes it. When she's put the children to bed and before she's ready for her own, he and she might smoke a cigarette and he might drink something. Maybe they'll both have a cup of tea.

It's the best room in the house, if you ask her. All so clever and light, fits together neatly, pulls out, drops down, folds away and slots into little gaps. Plenty of space and lots of cupboards, it makes her work in the house much easier. It takes enough time keeping this house nice as it is. She doesn't mind though. She doesn't have to work twice as hard to keep it clean like she did in their old place, doesn't have to worry about the people upstairs or next door. She doesn't have to make sure the sink is clean enough to use anymore. Her mum never had anything like this kitchen and never will. She loves it. It's so new-fangled and smart, she can look after the family all the better. She remembers that she was scared about moving all the way out here. So was he, she could tell, though he was set on it. It was the kitchen that settled her. He thinks about the future for them, he said that at the time, and she can see it now too. He could see how it would work out for us, wanted to get them away from town while they had the chance, he said. At first she thought, what's wrong with the old place? But she can see what he meant now and it's a fresh start in a completely new neighborhood where no one knows their business, where everyone has enough of their own space and wants to keep it nice. He talked her round, said he wanted her to know it was for the best too, to be behind him even though he'd do it anyway. They had to watch the pennies and tighten their belts to get this house but look at it! Look at her kitchen. She feels like a princess, right royally blessed. They couldn't have done better than this. Our little palace, he calls it.

See the children! In the sitting room two boys are looking a picture, as they say, like butter wouldn't melt, very neat and brushed, socks straight and laces tied, shirts tucked. You might imagine that they've been bribed to sit still with the promise that they can go and play in the garden in front of the house, even though they've had it drummed into them that they mustn't be a nuisance there either, because that they do share, with the other families in the road. She sits in an armchair opposite her husband. Her shy smile is an assurance of the complete perfection of the house and the life lived within it. She keeps a watchful eye to make sure the children are behaving.

Framed photographs sit on the mantelpiece, a family portrait and one each of the boys, and a vase on the folded-down dining table stands on a mat. A rug is set in front of the fireplace between the armchairs. In one of the recesses next to the fireplace a radiogram is parked. A corner of sideboard is the only other furniture visible in the room. The bay window is the perfect place to sit and watch the world go by. It's so peaceful, with a road that's no thoroughfare and the house set back from the road behind the front garden. This is the place where other times and places and other lives can be entered into through sanctioned pastimes like reading, and where horizons are broadened through the dimension of radio. In another 25 years or so this will be where the gaze of the family and its individual members can be opened up visually, through the worlds of television. A window to the exterior gestures towards a broader focus, offers a glimpse outwards to the wider world, shifting the gaze beyond the pull of the interior, turning players into audience.

Outside, Father busies himself in the shed. He stays there for hours, sorting, polishing, tidying, sharpening, cleaning, setting. When he's outdoors, his pipe is always at the corner of his mouth, unlit. The children weren't allowed in the shed at first. Now they can take him a cup of tea, all slopped over into the saucer and cold by the time they've got down there. The shed is his own space within the separate, private space he has engineered; like the kitchen is his wife's, he thinks. Everything has a place in there, like in the kitchen. It's an escape from the prim existence indoors that he has striven for and been maneuvered into. Only here can he truly organize his own time and space, where no one else needs to be considered, there's no family, house, tube train, or audience for his performance as father and worker. He thinks that it's the only place where he's really being himself, he thinks there's no stage here, not even a private one.

In the imaginary interiors of the living room stand mother, father and two children. At 2 Ennerdale Drive live two children, one mother and two aunties. They don't fit the bill of this stage set. They cannot play the roles allotted to this particular domestic stage, but here is where they live.

See Mummy! She waits for something. She sits and drinks to fill the time. She doesn't wave him off at the front door each morning or have a little break from her chores to sit opposite him when he arrives home at night. It's not what she expected. It's not what she hoped for. There are no bright lights in Colindale.

See the children! One son leaves as a young man to go and live in a city far distant in time and space; the other never moves away. One never comes back, the other never leaves.

● ● ●

It's their little palace, for sure, and a phrase that arises repeatedly in relation to the development of early-twentieth century suburbs. 'Little palaces' is a popular choice still for exhibition and book titles on the subject, and it appears in song lyrics and in railway publicity. From the heartfelt to the disparaging, its nuances run through the self-deprecatory to shades of smugness: an Englishman's home, our little palace, more than good enough for us. And haven't we done really quite well.

Emphatically not a flat, not 'rooms', but somewhere to be proud of, in a district close enough for travelling to work in central London and also for special outings to town. It's a place for people who are hard workers and who have been careful enough to put a little bit by. Laing's tackle the subject of exclusion themselves, in their neatly parceled up publicity: 'A house, a home, a little palace, in a convenient healthy district, purchasable by anyone with a small capital and regular income.' (John Laing & Co, 1930) A little palace is theirs for the asking. Other than transport and shopping information, Laing's provide no further details about the district. The emphasis is on the individual dwellings, not on the wider area. Later on, in the early 1930s, Laing's began to recognize and exploit the value in using local history and prominent figures to invoke the class credentials of an area in their publicity material and started concentrating on their public buildings. The unit here is still the single family. Rubbing shoulders is what's been left behind. Anyone else's little palace is their own affair.

The houses were chosen from a pattern book that showed the design variations in the housing that Laing's was building, produced by their small team of in-house architects under David Adam (1882–1953). Every one remains an individual dreamhouse with a nip and tweak here and there to differentiate it, however minutely, from the neighbors'. The red-shingled bay fronts of the redbrick villas in Colindale look like millions of others across north London. A site of imagined individuality, of supposed expression of personal taste outside urban constraints, in practice the suburban house was a series of shared reproductions. Though the details are all but absent in the publicity brochures, the 'total environment' was not ignored. Companies like Laing's took care of every aspect of estate development from site selection to landscaping and leasing of facilities.

John Laing himself was supposed to have an aversion to 'falseness' that has been attributed to his non-conformist background, and which translated visually into a lack of fake half-timbering and other such trickery in the houses designed by the company. It did not extend to the naming of places and house-types. Call it what you like but the suburbs didn't stint on the imaginary. With a rush of voluntarism, names were dreamed up to unleash the bucolic reveries of the potential homebuyer. Like nearby Mill Hill and Queensbury, Colindale enjoys a foundation in advertising fantasy. There is no dale. In the company biography by Berry Ritchie, Ennerdale Bridge in Cambria, Laing's childhood haunt on the edge of the Lake District, was noted as the probable source of the name.

Colindale and its neighbors constituted a watered-down suburban district, with a wink at the garden suburbs of Hampstead and Letchworth. Now middle- and working-class people could buy into a miniaturized and diluted version of the sylvan dream of unregulated, spacious living that had previously belonged only to the aristocracy and the upper classes. Colindale is no socially significant Port Sunlight in the Wirral, nor the architecturally distinct Hampstead Garden Suburb in London, nor Calcutta, where the first suburb was developed in 1770. Port Sunlight was planned to fulfill a set of philanthropic principles and to provide a residentially based community for the employees of a single industry, like Bournville and Cadbury's: 'In Chocolate Town all the trains are painted brown'. Elvis Costello's song 'Little Palaces' savages the philanthropic basis of such developments: 'It's like shouting in a matchbox made of plasterboard and hope.' Port Sunlight comprised a model village of 700 cottages and larger houses with schools, libraries, public buildings, canteen, shops and gym, conceived to harness the interests of the workforce to those of the industrialist. Bournville, like Hampstead Garden Suburb, was a publess paradise. In Colindale and similar suburbs the developer spotted a burgeoning new market coupled with a need and lubrication for social change.

Use of drive, grove, way, lane, crescent, gardens was considered more appropriate in suburban development than the far-too-mean 'street'. The names of the house styles were likewise selected for a particular national and aspirational appeal: Coronation, Jubilee, Olympia. Targeted buyers perceived a certain sort of Englishness brought back to the doorstep of their fantasy. Their style was imagined to rescue London from a perceived 'fog of colourless cosmopolitanism', which may indicate a dismissive xenophobia towards the proponents of then new International Style, many of whose champions were Jewish refugees from Europe. Quite a different expression of the zeitgeist was articulated than that visible in Ennerdale Drive, and both strongly epitomize their shared era.

Responding to and guiding the conservative preferences of customers fitted neatly with the developers' need to make quick return on their outlay. Demonstrably, this was a clear preference for most potential customers and fulfilling this was their best option, minimizing the risk of slower sales that might be the result of experimenting with modern design ideas and new technologies. The International Style wasn't for Colindale. The house at Ennerdale Drive might have constituted an event, but was never about being spectacular. The shortage of skilled plasterers and bricklayers between the wars was another circumstance that militated against new forms of house design. In order to address the rising cost and limited availability of building materials, Laing's developed in 1919 a system-built housing method called Easiform. This may also have been a response to the awareness displayed in the government-commissioned Tudor Walters Report of 1918 of the impact that the diminished pool of skilled labor would have on the success of the house-building boom. The report delivered a series of standards and specifications for the building industry and housing providers to follow in the postwar boom. Easiform was touted as 'a proved permanent form of in situ concrete house construction'. It would sidestep shortages of both materials and builders by allowing fast erection of houses by an unskilled labor force.

The pleasures of uncertainty might not be valued there but the suburbs embody enormous ambiguity: in their location, in their structure, in their design in their reference and in their materials.

Among its ambivalences, the suburban looks forward and back to two equally artificial vistas of a past that never was and a future that ignores the new. Suburban housing resolutely turns away from the new architecture and from the industrial technologies being exploited only down the road from Ennerdale Drive in the aircraft industry. The rows of semi-detached villas such as those erected in Ennerdale Drive marked an era of mass housing; the suburbs are an attempt at removal from time, through separation and refuge to slow down the brutal march of progress. In its time the suburban house was considered by some to be a badge of newness, and certainly sold as the future for the individual family.

The extent to which the suburban house is still read uncritically as a blueprint for English values, appealing to nostalgia and sentimentality is surprising. Its purchasers, who bought into their future with buildings of the past, are considered small-minded and parochial. That perceived 'inauthenticity', the labor-saving house clad in old-world clothing and the manufactured quality of the suburbs, is looked down upon as is the toy-town pastiche of suburban housing stock. As a response to the very idea of social aspiration, the critical reaction to suburban developments is mired in the very snobbishness that it criticizes: people should know their place.

In an attempt to provide different styles of housing, in 1935 John Laing launched a design competition jointly with the Architectural Association School of Architecture with the brief to design houses for the Sunnyfields Estate in Mill Hill in north London. John Laing offered this development site in order to underwrite this attempt to try to bridge what he saw as a gulf of 'mutual contempt between architect and builder'. The secondary aim of the competition was to stimulate interest among young architects in the 'somewhat peculiar requirements of building for direct sale and on designing for it,' as reported in the *RIBA Journal*, January 1936.

Five designers were selected to submit designs for the competition: the three student winners from the Architectural Association, Messrs Hyssop and Herbert and Miss Barker, were joined by Messrs Kenyon and Lloyd from Laing's, who also designed the estate layout. The key points of the brief for the designers to follow were that the houses must be 'villa-minded' (as distinct from a cottage or more 'municipal house') and should not be 'bizarre' or, in other words, not too modern. Up-to-date kitchen equipment and appliances however were considered 'crucial' for sales. Red or brown brick was specified rather than stocks (local, yellowish brick, prone to blackening with age), which were considered 'common', with colored pointing to contrast with the bricks; and facing bricks rather than stucco. Casement windows were valued over sashes.

The scheme was described in the *RIBA Journal* as having a unity, with bricks and tiles 'harmonious' and an 'unusual but composed' appearance. The differences between the models were said to be slight. Buyers were not convinced though and still plumped for the plainer and cheaper builder-designed houses, even though the design by the architects did not depart too radically from the firm's usual villa-style. 'This taste is certainly low … only an educated minority would prefer the architect-designed houses,' John Laing commented. He went on to express his disappointment at the public's conservative preference for 'ordinary type' houses. It is not clear whether the competition was considered fruitful at the time in promoting the desired understanding and collaboration between the professions, but its patrons counted it as a partial success at least. The houses, it was agreed, showed a refinement unusual in speculative development and Laing's intended to repeat the process with other young architects.

Exhibit 3: Lighting out for north London

The people who want to buy a house on Booth Road Estate can imagine the trees in the picture on the front of the brochure to be solely for their benefit. They may be wondering whether to embark on the enormous step of buying a house on this estate built by Laing's in 1930, quite probably their first house purchase. It may be a selling point to them that the open space outside their future front door is not open to all, that entry is restricted to Booth Road residents. Booth Road, not two miles from Ennerdale Drive, is close by the Grahame Park estate and leads into both Aerodrome Road and Aeroville, marking Colindale's aerial history with a mixture of the prosaic and the poetic. The foliage of trees covering two-thirds of the brochure cover softens the regimented sameness of the houses, which appear as a row

51

of identical sentinels in the distance, as though set back from the road. A cordon of green protects the houses and the space itself is secured from overuse and damage with chainlink fencing. That's belt and braces for you. If the standard suburban attraction of green space in front of the houses is closed off, whose trees are these? Anyone can look, a cat can look at a king but only the deserving few can touch. In a very strong sense the trees are window-dressing, crowding out the view and the page, nearby but unreachable, conveying the greenness and open countryside and wide vistas lacking in the city.

A second brochure for the same estate has a straightforward, no-nonsense cover showing the same local map as the first, narrowly defining the structure of the neighborhood exhorting the reader to 'Follow the Map for Laings Booth Road Estate Colindale NW9'. Inside, the copy plays up the economy and good value of such high-class housing. It's the estate with two tube stations for 'people of moderate means', which might mean working-class people moving into owner-occupation or families who would have been defined as lower middle-class.

The literature suggests that the sales staff were equipped to play a two-brochure routine to capture the starved urban hearts of potential buyers, assessing whether any particular customer would go for the romance and expansiveness of greenery or the hard measurable facts. What people want to know, or what Laing's wants them to know, is mostly about transport. The rates for quarterly season tickets – £2/17/6 (£2.77p) to Tottenham Court Road or Bond Street, £3/2/6 (£3.12p) to Bank – and 'useful information' about the cost of local rates, gas and 'electric current' – $3^1/_2$d (1.5p) per unit from North Metropolitan – are listed. The highest price of the three types of house available on the Booth Road Estate costs out at 26/8 weekly (£1.38) including all the rates. The weekly wage here is the 30/- mentioned earlier. Even allowing for contemporary equivalence, even at the lowest spec cost of 23/5, all in (£1.17), the sound of pips squeaking is almost audible. How much were those season tickets again? Its prominence in their publicity suggests that one of the main selling points for Booth

Road Estate is its closeness to transport facilities: only '2 minutes [sic] walk Colindale Stn', picked out along the bottom of the front cover, spelling it out because otherwise a potential vendor would never believe that transport could be so close. (The appeal of Ennerdale Drive was not proximity to the train station, a good half hour's walk from either Colindale or Hendon stations. No Daddy needed to rush off to work in that household.) Burnt Oak station is only five minutes away in the direction of Stanmore, to the north and the end of the tube line.

Continuing to extol the estate's appeal to the thrifty, the copy moves on to the benefits of local shopping parades, for this estate is pitched at people who are prepared to make the necessary cutbacks and scrimp to get to where they think they want to be, wherever they may be from. It then switches to the less measurable advantages of the development, explaining that the absence of terrace houses and consequent lack of overcrowding means fewer houses overall which will lead to faster sales to the lucky few only. Few means class, if you catch their drift. Few means scarcity value, in other words something hard to come by and sought after that everyone like you wants and will have and you need to have to continue to be one of these people. Early reservation is, as ever, advised. It is exclusivity that's being advertised. And exclusion must take place to achieve and maintain it. The leafy trees aren't going to get a look in here. This is the hard sell for the man of the house, who would be doing the buying. The trees and the kitchen appliances are for back-up appeal to his good lady.

The call to potential buyers' sense of economy continues with a page devoted to Laing's One Year Maintenance Policy, headed with a portrait of a solid and well-appointed pair of semi-detached houses. Those trees peeking through the background are oaks in connotation even if the quality of reproduction means that it's impossible to tell. At the foot of the page is a narrow picture of a local school, a proximity that continues to be a selling point. The maintenance policy, which Laing's is under no obligation to provide, is really a snagging notice for 'reasonable defects', but impressive nonetheless. An offer follows to delay hanging the wallpaper and applying the last coat of paint for up to 12 months after purchase; the maintenance policy also suggests that purchasers choose plain wallpapers in order to 'largely' prevent discoloring. The 1920s must have been a very damp decade. The itemization of prices promises 'no road or legal charges': Laing's hides conveyancing costs in the price, to make it easy. There's no hard negotiation necessary, this is the price. No need to do the sums yourself. Given the difficulties and the expense of printing, the inclusion in the brochure of house prices, utilities and season tickets in all their variations must be indicative of dormant inflation or speedy market turnover.

Elevated status is available with extras: 'extra frontage' is £5 per foot; corner sites command £30 extra; and a brick garage built on to the house is another £40, requiring an extra £10 deposit, as does the corner site property. The specification maps out exactly what people are getting for their money to encourage them to part with it, a series of well-researched and highly defined selling points lists some of the high spots from the double-depth foundations to the (obviously superior) English roofing tiles. The high-end spec house has heating in two of the three bedrooms and mantelpieces and tile surrounds in both reception rooms; outside woodwork in gloss paint; gardens fenced front and back; and the 11-inch cavity walls and facing brick for outside walls that were two of the cornerstones of Laing's reputation for quality development.

The extravagant itemization of reassurance goes further in a brochure for the more upmarket and 'moderne'- style Jubilee House with its curved metal-windowed bays and double-hipped roof. Here, 'Laing's features' that 'minimise maintenance costs' are numbered and illustrated 1–8 in yet another smartly designed diagram. The foundation trenches, accessorized by a solitary shovel left by a weary worker, are illustrated with a line drawing, as is the pouring of the ballast concrete into them; one man with wheelbarrow tips the stuff while another shovels it in. The painting of cast iron gutters is picked out to demonstrate the care given to the smallest detail, while the cavity walls, 'a definite guarantee against damp' (there's a rash statement in a northern

European climate), boast an airspace between their galvanized iron tiles of precisely two inches. Their damp proof courses, the cavity fair-faced brick walls, deep concrete foundations, wide eaves, oversized rafters and roofing felt under the tiles were all thought to be good practice unusual enough to warrant mention. Costain was another leading housebuilder of the time, and their company profile in property has been left behind too in favor of PFI projects, utilities and transport work. It was Costain, it transpires, that instigated cavity-wall construction, however often Laing's get the credit.

Laing's Queensbury Estate was presumably named after the boxing regulations, to benefit from the association with polite and gentlemanly conduct. Fair play! The estate is in Stag Lane, half a mile from Ennerdale Drive. The estate brochure makes its own appeal to the desires for thrift and aspiration of potential residents with a detached house on the cover and early mention of the cheapest suburban shopping center in this, the queen of northwest London suburbs. Only nine houses to the acre allows, it trumpets, more sunlight and more fresh air and better 'health'. This low density further improves on the recommendation of 12 houses to the acre made in the Tudor Walters Report.

With all the promised planting the completed estate would 'present the aspect of the park', a public amenity in a private setting. Top weekly price on the Queensbury Estate is 41/9 (£2.19) for a detached four-bedroom house with garage. A significantly later model (early 1930s) than Ennerdale Drive, the Queensbury houses boast 'outstanding' features, with a wider choice of decorations. This time the specifications are illustrated with a diagram that represents ideas through the imposition of a defining grid to classify data. A section through the house is surrounded by circles itemizing 'oak parquet hall floor', 'stout felt undertiles', superior fireplaces to choice' and so on.

The developers display their art in the power of association. Their pitch is a finely balanced appeal to regulate demand and sell houses, their literature carefully constructed and designed to tempt segments of the projected purchaser class. Despite its clear niche versions, itemized in full glory of their detail, they choose to include few representations of potential residents, no quotes from satisfied customers, no statistics, no shoutlines. No need: they know who they are.

The brochures' emphasis on practical details, especially the time-honored methods and value of materials going into the houses was decided upon at a time when, elsewhere, new materials were being put to new uses, towards other styles of domestic existence. No use was made in the houses in Ennerdale Drive of building materials such as iron and glass, to make possible diverse spatial organization, altering the separation of public and private space and of internal and external spaces. Even the street outside Booth Road Estate is made to look private, since no one is shown using it. The main, probably the only, innovative aspects of the houses in the bathroom and kitchen go unmentioned and it was largely in the kitchen where any technology was visible, in gas and electric appliances and the mechanics of folding tables and slide-out ironing boards. From landscaping to windows to furnishings, these buildings are closed up and designed precisely to enshrine the time-honored traditional roles played in the theater of the domestic.

Another example from a brochure by 'Britain's Best and Biggest Builders' New Idea Homesteads' used an image of a Puritan couple on the front, pioneers lighting out for the new territories in the mid 1930s. In case the company name doesn't make the point strongly enough, the cover image is strikingly unambiguous. The man dominates the space, almost cartoonishly large with chiseled cheekbones, enormous white collar and belt buckle. He looks toward the horizon, unknown and dangerous perhaps but everything in his demeanor declares it a prospect worth the struggle. His face is sunburned through hard outdoor work, as though he's been straining towards the heat of a new galaxy of prospects. The sword at his side is a guarantee of safety, against the need to beat off the common marauding hordes. One of his disproportionately large arms lies protectively around the shoulder of his wife. Her depiction adds little to the publicity value of the image and defies the general sentiment. Her whey-face is pinched, her hands clasped as if in prayer, her gaze more down her snub nose than towards the glorious prize of a semi-detached house. Behind the couple the masts and sails of Mayflower-like ships can be glimpsed (perhaps the new underground railway line was not functioning that day). At the edge of the beach by the moored ships stands a bare-chested, unkempt man in a pose that suggests he is someone unsuitable to be included in this golden dream, however much he might stride towards the foreground of the picture. New Idea Homesteads' housing designs include one named Arcadia, placing the emphasis unmistakably on the romance of the rustic idyll, hard-won for these putative suburb dwellers and all the more valued for that.

2 Ennerdale Drive and the millions of houses like it that appeared in the 1920s townscape was conceived as a sanctuary, you might imagine, against: the town, the neighbors, the missing family, the world. The house is the smallest unit in a battery of defenses against the dangerous modern world outside. Its windows, far from bringing the outside in, are to keep it safely away behind glass. They are for looking out from. Look at that! But you don't have to go there because you can see it all from here, through the wider view of the squared-off bay windows, looking almost round the corner. Far from the viewing mechanisms of the picture window and the film screen, the windows emulate the small divided panes of an earlier age, before technology made possible the manufacture of larger sheets of glass. The window breaks up the view into segments – shards of the outside world miniaturized into unthreatening sections. It's not about panorama, even though the view extends a long way. It includes the street, the garden, the sky, but all postcard-size. Small, safe missives from elsewhere. It's about staying in, keeping away, seeing what's coming, what someone else is doing. This is no accident: the design of the house is the framework for a lifestyle both public in the morning and evening march to the train station and private in the forms of domestic role-playing it instills. This is building as projection.

Window, house and neighborhood exist as barricade, a 'system of defense' against the exterior, as Beatrice Colomina describes it. Colindale is itself a barrier erected to keep the dramas of the wider world at bay, to refuse the encroaching dirt and sickness and overcrowding and depravity and noise of the city. It's not only the house that is a construct. The very tectonics of the house constitute an event: the event of suburban construction, a whisper not a fanfare. The building of the entire neighborhood is an artifice, created as proof against the encroaching massed humanity, the smells, the proximity of lives led inside the city. A more contained version of the domestic can then be ascendant, with the strict divisions needed to maintain distinction and distinctions.

The self-enclosed street layout at Ennerdale Drive, with broader streets and traffic circulation staggered through round-abouts, offers the quiet life as an attraction and is designed to the same purpose. The noise of other people's social interaction is a feature of urban existence that has been left behind. As a kind of precursor to the enforcement and development control of town planning, the Tudor Walters Report recommends street patterns rich in cul-de-sacs forming non-permeable neighborhoods where outsiders have no need to venture, as a planning response to the desire for privacy and peace and containment. Life in a newly developed suburb offered a multi-paned window of social anonymity, surely part of the attraction for those over-familiar with the private knowledge about other people's lives to which high densities and poverty gives access. The quiet life is an attraction for those whose lives have not been so quiet. As exclu-sivity shades into exclusion, the cul-de-sac becomes a dead end and a contemporary reading might see the cul-de-sac as inimical to the growth of a sense of community, and likely to provide the hidden spaces and opportunity for unwitnessed crime.

So it's not all chocolate. Publicity materials show selected constructions to represent and define acceptable forms of domestic (life) arrangements in the new suburban life and choose what to leave unsaid, and unrepresented. Little palace and suburb, heartland or hinterland, home isn't always so cozy despite its connotations of shelter, safety and warmth, of being 'at home' sharing cups of tea and secrets. Home truths hit home telling people they're no better than they should be. The passage of time can harden an attitude of exclusivity into a position of exclusion, can change an understandable desire for safety and privacy into restricted access. That 'healthy district' promised in Laing's brochure copy goes beyond the guarantee of much-needed good sanitation. Like the frequent references in the literature to 'hygiene' and 'drainage', the phrase is a coded promise to leave undesirable (read: dirty, poorer than you) neighbors behind. The maintenance of exclusionary boundaries between the us and the them assures purchasers that the area is kept safe and clean for those who are meant to be there. Those who are not are fenced out, literally and economically.

Designed to appeal to a promise of exclusivity the suburbs clearly were, but the need for the 'healthy district' also had some basis in newly available information about the effects of poor environment on health exposed in First World War recruitment halls, the 'twin evils of vice and ill health in towns' as Robin Evans describes it. The number of would-be soldiers whose health problems disqualified them from service was considered to be disturbingly high, and also revealed wide disparities of health levels between classes. Robin Evans is referring here to an earlier manifestation of domestic architecture as social control, from the 1840s. He describes how the Victorians saw a close connection between substandard housing and low morality, one they believed might be broken through the provision of better housing and improved employment prospects. This particular wave of suburbia in the 1920s was sold to willing takers partly through veiled references to health and hygiene; in time, the connection between environment and health was joined with supporting design principles. The modern movement is more explicitly linked with radical ideas about cleanliness and fresh air and marked with design motifs of sunbursts and the clean fresh lines of flat-roofed houses and flats.

Low density and indoor plumbing are some of the effects and trappings of the new housing in bathrooms and bedrooms. These in turn allowed the culturally prized separation of toileting and washing and sufficient space for gender segregation of siblings. Shifting the stage of daily life indoors away from the public gaze, taking what was exterior to the interior and having an indoors to enclose private family life, is more than a mark of moving up the social scale. All these features were equated with a sense of moral as well as bodily cleanliness and imbued with enormous cultural and class value, quite apart from the improvement to living conditions which is to be celebrated. The Tudor Waters Report recommended that new houses should be built with a bathroom, although at the lower end of the speculative house building trade price dictated that bathrooms and toilets were combined. This was a move that cut down on costs for stud walls, doors and tiling, as well as reducing contract time. Speculative builders were not tied to Tudor Walters' standards as providers of municipal housing were, and could dilute its proposals in terms of space and structures. Cost proved more important than installing the means of cleanliness and morality for the lower orders.

Housing design can set in brick gender and class roles and relations. Despite being mired in ambiguity on some levels, the houses are a physical manifestation of the fine distinctions of class, throwing them into sharp relief. This effect is not only evident in the obvious markers like the size of the house but also in such details as whether the house boasted a one- or two-storey bay which revealed at which end of the market a property sat. In an exteriorization of the external, the houses are designed to enforce and extract a particular performance of domesticity within a territory of exclusion, their structures and definitions predicated on notions of whose 'place' it is to live there. The suburbs' strenuously gendered image, where women stay in and men commute, is something of a suburban myth. The suburban life may be characterized by stratified gender roles, and women were expected to play an ever-present domestic role, performance aside, but women worked in greater numbers outside the home than they had before the First World War.

The impact of changes in the mortgage market was matched by an influx of women in jobs and industries that had previously been solely male preserves: in the newly expanded factories, and from the beleaguered end of the middle classes. An increase in household income both encouraged many people to buy into the property market and was also essential to be able to make that move. Whether or not it was the need for income to meet the mortgage that meant women had to work, the image of woman at leisure remained; indeed it needed reinforcement and posters to prove it. Mortgages were not necessarily easy to pay, and they were not necessarily easier for everyone to get either. Even if the Ennerdale Drive aunties were over 30 years of age in 1918 they would only have enjoyed the right to vote for less than ten years when they bought the house. It wasn't until ten more years passed that women in England were granted equal voting rights with men. The aunties may have needed a man to front the house purchase for them since women remained legal and financial minors. Women needed permissions and signatures from male guarantors to expedite transactions or contracts and also to grant them respectability.

As front garden separates front door from the street: as hall separates us from them again, the ubiquitous serving hatch between kitchen and dining or living room in suburban houses operates as the marker of transformation of kitchen worker into hostess. The recommendation in Tudor Walters that each house should have a scullery as well as a kitchen and larder was supposed to make it easier for the woman without servants to run her own kitchen. It also provided a spatial separation to indicate that the kitchen was no longer for dirty work, which was relegated to the scullery. If middle-class women had to take on the housework previously subcontracted to servants, the image and practice of housework and its main space in the kitchen had to reflect this. The site of this non/work had to be transformed from the high-windowed, badly ventilated area that was considered fit for servants into a place of light, airy atmosphere. The kitchen had to be brought into the home as a room where good things happened, turned into a place where the woman of the house worked while also promulgating the idea of housework as leisure and so an activity that took place outside of 'work'. This image was popularized through the provision of professional house-cleaning tools, and the labor-saving kitchen designed to take the drudgery out of caring for the family.

Suburbia is made up of family units devoted to the minutiae of their own seemingly never-ending and at once fascinating and interminable relational dramas. In this sense suburbia achieves the widely held idea of a uniform state of identical houses, streets, neighborhoods, families. In relation to the details of its actual, physical housing and attendant social standing, such an idea is wildly inaccurate and absurd. Housing design in the suburbs encompasses tudor- or jacobethan, georgian, moderne, neo-vernacular, even mansion blocks of apartments. The design of the house might incorporate pebbledash, half-timbering, metal windows, leaded panes and lights, brush-grained woodwork, contrasting mortar, red facing bricks, render-hung tiles, curved bays. 2 Ennerdale Drive does not display all of these markers, any more than its inhabitants conform to the family of convention to fit the suburban stereotype. Critics might contend that suburban life's performance of the past in the present takes place in a house like a play house, a child-like model of what a house is and should be, as well as a playhouse. A facsimile of house, its inhabitants are not only playing their roles on a set, they are also watching themselves do it, smiling, with self-approval. Or is that uncertainty?

Laing's publicity copy is riddled with clues and hints about what's being sold and to whom. The company proved itself to be highly skilled at providing for, and also shaping and influencing, the prevailing tastes of the time: architectural, environmental, financial and aspirational. What's missing and left unspoken gives away as much as what's included, or more. Fear lies beneath its offer and its attraction, and fear drives the good train Enterprise and the depth and breadth of the fear is why it's deliberately and understandably left unsaid. 2 Ennerdale Drive is a house created in but not of the modern age and it reflects the fragility and insecurity of such a position. New residents of the suburban palaces can gratefully turn away, indoors, from the uncertainties of the postwar climate, the horrors of the recent war, the hardships as the country heads into recession. Their fears of the future and the past, of a loss of place and fear of change, of a tenuous class position in a shifting terrain, spur a desire for security and normalcy, met by the safety of the housing design of the suburbs.

Lloyd George's Homes for Heroes slogan, coined to popularize a postwar house-building initiative, is widely recognized as more than social improvement masquerading as gratitude. Rather it presents a mix of good intention and expediency, handily providing housing close to industrial centers for manual workers, while their white-collar counterparts might easily access desk jobs in the city of London. Everyone can get to work to earn the money to pay the mortgage. The house in the semi-rural idyll is a reward for the privations of the First World War, a fearful bribe against radical action and the socialist menace and a buffer against the social upheaval of the forthcoming General Strike and Second World War. Speculative builders like John Laing & Co were keen to make use of legislative change and financial freedoms and provide the housing needed for the still young century. They tapped into and exploited the global and local insecurities of the day by colluding and delivering illusion of certainties about the roles and entitlements in suburban life.

The house is the site of the family, and the purveyor of respectability. Residents and authorities have in common a fear of eruption, the surfacing of the underside, of what's excluded in order to guarantee that social conformity. This is depicted, across the distance of several decades and the Atlantic Ocean, grotesque and effective in the pulsating suburban lawn in David Lynch's film *Blue Velvet*. Any danger or threats to this idyll are from outside the walls, beyond the boundaries. Elsewhere is, by definition, a danger. Father's role as protector is crucial. Safe as houses, that's how he likes it. While his wife is busily making the daytime safety, making the family that makes safety too, he and she together as a combined force repel the dirt, the dark, the things where they shouldn't be. He growls around the home, having relocated it far enough away from city dangers and delights of sex and drink and violence and anonymity. Over his dead body, he thinks.

Chapter 3

Missing persons

And where is daddy? He's not at 2 Ennerdale Drive. Maybe he's never been there. As the great-aunties of his son Antony moved into their house in the new suburbs and as another son, Richard, was in his first season at the Old Vic Theatre in Waterloo, Henry Ainley was returning to the stage ten miles away in the West End of London. After a two-year absence due to a breakdown and lengthy convalescence, Henry remains secure enough in his position that no visual reminder is needed to promote himself in the newly published *Spotlight*. Henry's entrance in his comeback appearance in The First Mrs Fraser at the Theatre Royal in Haymarket was met with several minutes of show-stopping applause. The story goes that he broke both his big toes in an accident when he fell off the stage but another version has it that the fall happened during his convalescence. His complicated private life involved his mistress, a divorced Baroness from the US via a marital home in Germany; a marriage in freefall with offspring and (at least) two 'love children' to provide for; and an alcohol problem more than whispered at. Poor darling. His was a sorry and comic predicament such as might have befallen Melchior Hazard, the pater familias from Angela Carter's *Wise Children*, a portrait of another, more fictional, acting dynasty. The theater is all for Melchior Hazard too, who is drunk on his own myth, and the novel is a fantastic, quasi-Shakespearean romp of multiple sets of brothers and twins of uncertain parentage, mistaken identity, jealous siblings and foundlings and it's all very familiar.

The suburban life is not for Henry. Suburbs are about keeping yourself to yourself; 2 Ennerdale Drive presents itself quietly. There's no theater nearby that he knows of. The suburban life is not for the likes of any of them: two spinster aunties, one unmarried mother, two absent fathers, one son emigrated, one unmarried. It's not the place for them but there they lived for 80 years. The suburban life was never quite the simple, homogenous affair of identical family groups settled within the appropriate suburb to their income and class status but appearances have to be maintained. A poor fit of socio-economic location to circumstance it may have been, but that duration of residence is one measure of the extent of their discomfort. The stage of suburban life is too narrow to accommodate Henry, or maybe there's too much open space for him. The domestic stage at no.2 exists within and without the house. Later on, members of this in-house cast were to exit nightly to play elsewhere, in the world of exchange and commerce. For now, it's the life within that the characters attend to inside 2 Ennerdale Drive during the long days and nights. Hush, it's private, detective.

No greater drama takes place than that on the stage in the theater of family, where people are born and live and die. Henry knows that, even if there's no playhouse in Colindale. Keep it in the family. One-off and unrepeatable, the same scenes are being presented and viewed, over and over, up the road, round the corner, across town, across all the towns. Henry knows too about the compulsion to repeat: the unending performance, on stage and off, the constant portrayal and acting out; the applause; the depression.

Wherever the family and the family home are sited, castle or little palace, the non-stop drama of the domestic needs a setting. The promise of suburban life meant moving the theater of family and local life into the domestic interior; greater privacy within the home meant separation and distance from the more public life of the exterior. In the theater of the domestic, family members supply a pre-formed, resident company of characters. The suburban house might be an embodiment of the desire for a seamless, unambiguous existence but it's the location of an eternal soap, a docudrama with stalwart characters. Supporting artists and understudies come center stage without warning or plot device and the others, the sword carriers and bit-part players, fall into family and dramatic life for a time, then out again.

Characters serve as spectators and players, watching their own story dramatized in the house, for their eyes only. This domesticity is a performance whose audience may not exist beyond its own players. An unseen performance is its own reward, like virtue; it plays out what is defined and demanded by the bricks of its unseen domestic stage. The intention in developing the early twentieth-century suburbs was never to create an experimental stage to try out new forms of production; the suburb was designed around an ideal of enclosure and a coercion of the town planning and architectural arts. The intention was rather to set up standard plot lines, in a culture refusing deviation from the script.

In the public theater the roles of spectator and player are fixed in time, duration and space and are usually both scripted and choreographed. The theater player is bound to act a role from its beginning to its end, maintaining continuity with their character. That much is clear. Audiences come and watch the players at the theater; they are self-selected and then share together the experience of witness and response. Their involvement in the performance is invaluable. Without them, there is only rehearsal. The mushrooming of media and forms of entertainment has changed the experience of theater and film acting almost beyond recognition since Henry's heyday. Yet some aspects of the nature of celebrity are unchanged: the ubiquity and easy casting of stars in particular types of role for box-office returns; the bravura performances; the looks and fan-base; the demand for voice-over talent. Reviews invariably stress Henry Ainley's good looks, his beautiful speaking voice and his charm. Revered as an actor, Henry was also adored as a matinee idol. Even in the briefest online biographies, it is always deemed to be worth including the information that Henry began his four-decade-long career as an amateur. He's a natural, an untrained savage who came from nowhere (otherwise known as a drama group in Yorkshire). The currency of the transformational narratives which now fill TV schedules and print media is a durable one.

Despite Henry's 40 years on the stage the Ainley dynasty turned out to be a minor act among more active and enduring acting families, though it has included four generations so far: grandfather, great aunt, uncle, father, brother, sister, cousin. John Laing's family is described as the 'Laing dynasty of British builders' with only two generations mentioned, although several more must have been involved, founded as the company was in 1848. The Ainley acting dynasty can't quite match the social respectability of their two knighthoods, either. The channels of familial and artistic descent run deep and shallow, criss-crossing and leaping generations like red hair.

Henry's social position starts and ends in places she'll never see, whether as detective or grand-daughter: from the Yorkshire mines where his father worked to the high society circles that he moved in as a leading actor of his day. Actors like him *were* high society with the privileges of privacy that accrued in an era before the explosion of the cult of celebrity personality and its concomitant private-as-public effect had all but replaced public life. Henry and his peers were able to lead wild lives in an era prior to the democratization of the post-Second World War period and the social changes of the 1960s. Before private lives became the stuff of public record and private lives the fodder for unabashed public appetites, 'his flawed greatness', the details of his affairs and his messy private life might have been common knowledge but a respectful distance was maintained.

Ethel Hardie's unpublished biography *Henry Ainley: Portrait of a Great Actor* would be an entirely straightforward theatrical biography, a gazetteer of the work of Henry Ainley and an almanac of English theater in the 1920s and 1930s, had author and subject not been related by marriage. She was Richard Ainley's first wife and in the business herself. The material in her book is an invaluable source for this work: one professional with the insider family knowledge of the daughter-in-law writing about another insider. It's not an act she could follow here. One reason, she was told, that Ethel did not seek publication for her highly informative work was the fear that 'things' would be misinterpreted. 'Things' like a sheaf of letters from Henry to Laurence Olivier which might be interpreted by the theater critics in such a way that the public would conclude that the two had been engaged in a sexual affair. Which, it seems, they had.

She'd never heard a whisper until she read a book review in the national press over breakfast one morning. That's public for you. It was difficult enough already to keep up with Henry's wives and mistresses without adding the complications of an illegal same-sex affair. She wasn't in the profession, she wouldn't know. If there was any doubt, defensive denials from both families had an opposite effect to that intended and stamped the stories as true. The letters are in the Laurence Olivier Collection in the British Library and available for anyone to read. The two of them filmed *As You Like It* together in 1936/37 and the letters leave little doubt that during that time they were passionately connected. 'Henrietta' and 'Larrikin' sound feverish, coy, flirtatious, petulant and puppyish by turns; the letters are full of detail about theater business, professional competition ('I shall soon be back and acting you into the orchestra'); and mentions of wives in an 'o how she must hate me' kind of way. And it's this last that probably accounts for the extent of the disbelief, homophobia aside. Both men were multiply married, and Olivier was at the time married to Vivien Leigh! So how could that happen?

Reading the letters to Laurence Olivier was painful, but it had to be done. So much lost information, so many closed avenues, it would have been foolish to ignore them. Except it didn't feel like looking, it was peeking. Reading (love) letters written by someone to whom you're related is a grossly prurient activity, not as squeamish as it would be to read your parents' letters, but much more so than knowing intimate details about celebrities you'll never meet (and he's one of those too).

What makes it interesting is that it took 60 years after Henry's death and 15 after Laurence Olivier's in 1989 for this 'revelation' to appear in print. It's hardly man bites dog: two successful, attractive, professionally powerful men in the theater fit in an affair alongside their serial heterosexual engagements. Neither man had a reputation for sexual continence, and by some accounts Olivier struggled throughout his life to contain his sexual feelings for men. One stage further on from outright denial that any affair took place, the pernicious idea was touted that Henry, the older man, had somehow preyed upon Olivier's young gorgeousness. This is to forget that Henry too had been tagged in his day 'the most beautiful man in London' (more baton-passing then) and years of drinking hadn't entirely extinguished his charms. Following that came the homophobe's retreat, that this was a one-off aberration. But the idea that Henry was the only one and a predator at that doesn't really stand up either. A very limited amount of research reveals claims that Danny Kaye, the American actor and entertainer, also had an affair with Olivier.

The Laurence Olivier archive also tells her that Henry was talking about Richard to Olivier in 1936, though in a somewhat disconnected way ('How does my son Richard shape as a performer?'). So by his late 20s, Richard, who began his stage career using the more anonymous second name Riddle rather than Ainley, was recognized publicly as Henry's son. She'd heard it said that Henry had chosen to acknowledge paternity through the intimacy of an introduction to his tailor on Jermyn Street in Piccadilly when Richard was already a young man. She thought this an event hilariously and tragically like a scene from *Upstairs Downstairs*, a 1970s television series about life above and below stairs in Edwardian London, in which Antony later appeared. In another letter to Olivier dated 1938 Henry reports that 'Richard says he is a better actor than either you or I', so Richard must have felt close enough to his father by then to indulge in some theatrical bluster of his own. Further, Ethel Hardie's biography reports that Henry had pleaded with the mother of Richard and his sister Henrietta to marry him, when the two offspring were grown up enough to hear and be amused. One anecdote might appear to confirm another here: the story of paternity acknowledgement in adulthood.

Henry was the brightest star of the Ainley acting firmament. Although he is barely known outside acting circles today, he is the source of the 'distinguished theater background' cited in Ant's obituaries. Ant's role as The Master, the villain in the BBC series Dr Who 'lurking in the shadows with a cat-like purr, a malevolent chuckle and a predilection for sadism' from 1981 to 1989 made his career. It was Ant who was responsible for killing off Dr Who played by Tom Baker, an ex-pupil of her dad's who had lived with them for a time and whom she had adopted as her godfather. Ant was still in the role when the program was cancelled and it was a Dr Who tour that he was about to go on when she spoke to him in the 1990s. Ant's obituary in *The Times* called his character 'A threat to the known Universe'; his catch-phrase was 'I am the Master and you will obey me.' She'd always thought 'anyone for tennis' was more his line, with his roles in *Upstairs Downstairs* and as the Reverend Emilius in *The Pallisers*, a 1974 adaptation of the Anthony Trollope books.

'Anyone for tennis' was Ant's line in his private life, not professionally. He hadn't made a career out of it, he *was* it. He wore sports jackets and spoke in a rich, actorly fashion, an updated version of his father's mahogany tones. Those roles and his general demeanor had stayed with her. The rest of his career gives quite a different picture, with bit parts in films and series too adult for her to understand then: *Oh What a Lovely War!* (she liked the songs); *You Only Live Twice* (boys' stuff); *Spyders Web*, a 1970s series she barely remembered though he was the lead; and Dr Who, which she never saw him in, considering herself too old to watch when he was in it in the 1980s. Then, by the time Dr Who had been repackaged as retro-cool culture and started broadcasting again in 2005, Ant was dead and present only in re-runs; The Master was recast with Derek Jacobi and then John Simm.

It was the 1960s when she knew Ant. He was already a grown man and didn't embrace being part of that era as a younger man might have done. In her memory he was too old for the 1960s but still someone who lived in his time, rather than being old and foreign enough to ignore local contemporary culture like her parents were and did. He looked modern, if not groovy, and hung out with a swinging London set. He was 'shockingly glamorous', so The Sis told her, some 40 years later. She imagined he might have smoked a little hash, or maryjane as he might have called it, though alcohol was the family preference he shared. He spun round town in his brown Mini thrillingly faster than anyone she knew drove then, and older family members routinely refused to accept lifts with him. He was a betting man and he abandoned her in the car alone more than once, while he went to pay a visit to 'my friend Joe Coral', leaving her free to play with the controls on the dashboard, and scare herself by experimenting with the handbrake and the ignition. It only took a few minutes for him to nip in and place a bet. Ant didn't introduce her to his friend Joe and he never visited him for long. The car jerked downhill, just enough to put her off doing it again, until the next time.

'Actor and cricketer' his obituaries say, suggesting that he was as committed to his cricketing career as he was to his acting. Even when Ant wasn't resting he found the time to be tennis coach in a prep school (brown bonnets) up the road from her primary school (green berets). But it was Dr Who, not sport, that bagged him the surprisingly extensive obituaries in the national press. Surprising to her that is, because of her ignorance about his career-defining role in a program that bestows almost instant national-treasure status on its participants. She didn't even know about his public life.

Father and son shared a passion for cricket too. Ethel Hardie's biography of Henry describes how he had once risked and received a leathering from his mother, the scary-sounding Ada, for skipping school so that he could carry the bag of Yorkshire cricketer Bobby Peel at his benefit match in Leeds. Cricket was a life-changing pastime for Henry. He auditioned for Frank Benson's theater company when his experience was limited to the Sheffield Casuals Amateur Dramatic Society and work as an extra in a Leeds production of Henry Arthur Jones' *The Masqueraders*. Asked by the man himself, known as The Sportsman, what his favorite sport was, Henry's enthusiastic response clinched the deal and landed him his first professional job.

Exhibit 4: Henry Ainley (1879–1945) twice

'Mr Henry Ainley' it reads. The name is reversed out of the image in white in an art nouveau-style typeface, in caps and small caps. This modestly sized title sits at the bottom of the portrait, with a little curlicue at the end of the name even though it would be more legible in the white unprinted band at the bottom of the portrait. The title begins at the point where the curve of the right cuff disappears behind his wrists and stretches across to the besuited crook of the left elbow.

He stares ahead determinedly. Arms folded, he's restrained, holding himself back with the stance of a forthright manly man. Fashions change and folded arms are more likely now to be read as bullish, yet withholding: a negative take on containment. Either way, it's a pose of non-participation. Staring, not smiling, this one's not giving much away. A crescent of eyewhite shows beneath his pupil and gives an

impression of fearfulness. Studiedly without expression, he's in suit and tie, handkerchief in pocket. Is he trying to look serious, less like a pin-up boy, or is that a role he grew into along with his matinee-idol reputation? A stripe is evident in the weave of his shirt on the inner cuff, which is not visible on the outer side. His tie sits at the base of a detachable, fold-down Albany collar, in a double round knot.

Whoever he is, 'Henry Ainley' has autographed the card slant-wise. This is him. The title and the signature guarantee it. The photographic medium bestows upon him the means of escape: he is represented in performance. It's him and not him. There is no 'conquest' of his 'incognito'. It is for this reason that a photograph is a space of disappearance, not only because what it portrays is gone forever already. His signature is barely legible since it falls across the dark fabric of his suit except for one descender of the *h* and part of the *e*, with long cross strokes on the *H* and the *A*. The ink has faded and the script is barely visible. It's a hand more open and clear than any I've ever seen in other family members' handwriting. The example I saw of my dad's writing as a younger man in the Olivier archive in the British Library was like a new hand to me, almost unrecognizably legible. Henry's letters in the archive are written in a much more scrawly hand than his postcard sample, but then the letters weren't addressed to me. An autographical signature is a performance in itself, delivered to an audience or witnessed by its receiver.

The postcard has slightly rounded corners. Both signature and paper surface are matt; a shininess has formed in areas where the card is bent or scratched. Tiny pieces of emulsion have chipped off. Assuming it was produced during his lifetime, the postcard is at least 70 years old. The portrait shows Henry in his early career, when he was still a young man but the vanity of choosing out-of-date youthful self-portraits means that any correlation between his age and the date of production of the postcard is hard to judge.

Photographic portraits of famous performers were one of the postcard format's original applications when it appeared in the early 20th century. The postcard is big enough to see the face properly and small and light enough to carry on your person. The signature across the front suggests he was sending them out as a response to fan mail or giving them away to stage-door devotees. A production line, an audience of thousands and an individual one-off special from (I'm guessing) him to her, from you to me, signed and in my pocket. A portrait brings both distance and closeness. He speaks to me. That's me he's talking to. It's an early form of merchandising, a keepsake for fans in an age of fewer means of reproduction, with scant technology to re-view, re-listen. Perhaps this portrait was released when he was in a popular show; perhaps it was a calling card when he was visiting agents or directors; perhaps it was part of a series, like football cards or Pokemon. It's an item of wide circulation, a printed item rather than a multiple print of a photograph like a carte de visite. For a devoted fan this postcard would have been currency at the time and a valuable signed photographic postcard held all the dearer. It may have been a card that a fan brought to him for autograph. Which way did this exchange take place? And how did I come to have it?

Photographic portrait cards of performers produced now still tend towards the retro: Humphrey Bogart, Clara Bow, James Dean, names from the period of huge Hollywood studios. If they're more recently famous or still working, you can see them hear them read them in their own medium and then across others too: in downloads, in the print and digital press, on TV and radio. Henry did his share of radio interviews and who knows what counted for over-exposure in an age before proliferation and saturation? Him again!

It's a postcard that's designed to be sent, to another fan ideally. This copy is blank on the back, the non-image side, which has only the standard printings:

Postcard

The address to be written on this side

POST CARD.

Printing 'postcard' twice on an item that is plainly a postcard seems an unnecessary incongruity and results from compliance with a code of postal service charges. The Royal Mail granted permission to manufacture picture postcards that could be sent through the post in 1894. Designed to be sent without an envelope, a postcard is both lighter and less bulky than a letter and was therefore cheaper to send. Before email and SMS usurped it, the postcard was correspondence of choice for the more disposable end of postal communications. You're making a point now if you send a letter and even the ephemeral postcard has again become special, no longer of the everyday, to the distress of the postal services. This example comes from a German company based in London, 'Published by Giesen Bros and Co, London EC.', and was produced in Berlin. Printing abroad wasn't unusual; postcards had been produced in Europe since 1870.

The postcard settled in the market as a mass-produced item used as a gift exchange of short-form correspondence of a leisure-style informality, most often of roughly A6-size (105 x 148mm), although 'court' (115 x 89mm) and 'intermediate' (130 x 80mm) sizes also used to exist as postcards. Due to its brevity and the unsealed quality of its message, nothing of a private or legal nature can be written on it. When

looking at a postcard addressed to someone else there's a performance of averting the eyes from the not-very-private-at-all correspondence of another person, enacted through a perceptible lowering of
lids or narrowing of focus necessary to read the information on the
back and nothing else. 'Where is this lovely place? I'd like to go there
too.' 'I've been there, what's it called again?' At the same time the
performance involves being seen to not read the message that
somehow, despite being open and uncovered, is supposed to be for the
eyes of the recipient only. Sending postcards as holiday missives or
billets doux is a modern practice: this one was meant to be read. 'Look
what I've got', just as the postcard from elsewhere else says, 'Look
where I am. (But I'm thinking of you.)' Or at least, 'I'm reminding you
where I am'.

The number 7938 is printed in the bottom right-hand corner,
slightly lower than the name but set in an equally prominent though
different typeface. Who knows what the number relates to. It could be
a negative number, part of the studio's categorization system, or it
might relate to the printer's series of postcards or a number in a print
run. There's no photographer's credit, no indication of who took the
portrait. Later in his career Henry visited renowned portrait photog-
raphers in specialist studios who automatically had a credit attached.
Cecil Beaton is a name I'd expected to turn up. Henry started young
and made his name early so a self-financed visit to a high street practitioner is still possible.

Henry is standing at a quarter turn from the camera; in full view are
the straightness of his nose, deep-set shaded eyes, a rather plump
jawline, full lips and firmly marked philtrum, characteristics that mark
several of his descendants. The definition of his eyes is strong and dark.
I suspect a touch of kohl on the inner lash line. Of Irish and Yorkshire
parentage, descriptions of Henry's looks were often prefaced with
'exotic', and were considered to be so unusual in England that some
thought a mixed-race background could be the only possible cause.

I find a second postcard. This one is a more stylized image generally,
framed by a white border. The same background sheet, the same

darkness around the eyes, deep-set in their shadows, the same set of the shoulders, but while the face is fully in profile, his head is angled slightly upward, looking into the distance. It would be a slightly awkward pose especially for long exposures. He looks younger, stands taller in the image. While the first postcard is in a soft brown-toned black, this second postcard has a slight magenta cast to it, which gives a feverish tone to the skin, a youthful wash of flush and bluster. Being shown entirely in profile like horseflesh is not to his best advantage but fills the frame to the top and a stronger sense of presence is the result, which is everything. Otherwise the only gain is more suit. More suit means that the entirety of the deeper and longer cut of the lapel can be seen. There's a lavish width of the dinner jacket's satin-faced lapel in contrast with the rather sober narrowness of the suit jacket in the first postcard.

The camera used for this image would have been a bulky large-format apparatus, the portrait a slow process, and readable in the ponderous formality of the finished work. Henry looks carved in marble, which is to say immobile. It's an image that a fan could forever cherish as unchanging. It might denote a conglomeration of the professional talents of photographer and actor for composure and stillness and for capture and rendering on photographic paper. A relationship must have existed between the intentions of photographer and subject, however momentary, in the making of this portrait. Their art and guile came together in a joint effort, magnifying the parts into a greater sum, an alchemic trickery of silver particles instead of gold. This may not be the first postcard but it is certainly one of many made of Henry Ainley. Later on, this formal if not stiff pose would give way to the contrived informal or character shot.

There is shadow only around the eye sockets. The skin is thick and smooth, unlined except for the beginning of a frown mark at the inner corner of his eyebrow, it's without tone or definition. A slight shadow between the outer edges of nose and mouth indicates the onset of ageing. The waves in his hair are coiled like rope, the whorls sculpted with oil or pomade. All the surfaces appear planed and flat, except for the raised, almost corded, texture of his suit. The stormy backdrop brightens on the left of the postcard as if the clouds by his ear are clearing by the side of his nose. The texture of the studio background works to enliven the portrait, giving a depth and a dimensionality to it.

As his shoulders are turned slightly more to front, the V of his waistcoat, the shirt front, collar and tie are all easily discernible. This time he's in an Ascot collar, which leaves both the tie knot and the circle of tie around the collar open to view. It's somewhere between a tie and a cravat, fittingly more formal with the suit and pose. This collar suits his build far better. The high-cut collar of the first postcard gives an impression of a stolid stockiness. A contemporary sensibility alerts the viewer to the discomfort that such a collar must cause, a restriction in mobility of the neck and so in physical expression. The constriction of those folded arms, as any actor would tell you, is inimical to the unimpeded passage of the breath necessary to be in good voice. And without his voice, how does any actor leave his mark? The downward glance is further suggestion that a turning in rather than out is taking place in this presentation of his image for an audience of thousands. He's caught in the tightness of a conventional pose struck for a portrait session. A bank clerk in early life, he was no stranger to formal wear. The second postcard shows an elegant expanse of neck, elongated out of the collar, and the raised jawline parallel to the collar edge is a further improvement to his presentation. The contrast of tone in the flesh is such that both jawline and neck are visible in the smaller image, while the first shows an undefined wall of flesh and a doughy excess where a bone should be.

His nose in full profile forms a perfect isosceles triangle. It could almost be prosthetic, paler than the rest of the face and unshadowed; too much highlighter perhaps. No kohl this time, judging by the definition of the eye. His hair, in the first picture so molded, looks wild and ungreased. It's longer, with unruly front edges and straighter back. He looks quite the Prince Hal in waiting (or do I think that because the Hardie biography informs me that Henry V was his first major Shakespeare role, in 1900?).

The white border dates the card between 1916 and 1930. The title on the card is printed along with the identifying numbers and other information (likely to be the name of the photographer but it's too small to read) appears in a stripe of non-image white at the bottom. There's no signature here, just the name printed in decorative uppercase script followed by an unnecessary full stop.

There's no shortage of material about the working lives of Henry and other family members, available thanks to a constellation of technologies and era-appropriate methods of access. No detection is necessary, the world heaves with data. Their lives are particularly well documented with playbills and pictures of their faces captured onstage and on camera and the British Library Newspaper Archive in Colindale is the repository for press coverage about all of them. If the Ainley dynasty had begun when Laing's did, there'd be no moving footage and no sound recording. Technologies from Henry's era enforce a separation between sound and image. Within the copious representations available of him, sound and image are amply covered but not together, not running at the same time, and not from the same source. He is a man of parts, a voice and a face. His real home is indeed the stage, where his constituent attractions come together to form a man famed for acting, speaking and beauty. He inhabits the stage, completely and complete. Playing roles may be insubstantial in their temporariness but the recordings and representations of them have long lives, as long at least as the primacy of the technology used to play or view them. With the accelerated lives of technologies in the century or so since Henry's career began, some of the material is lost in irrecoverable formats such as unplayable Ferrograph reel-to-reel recordings and worn out and stretched tapes and disks. Henry's film debut was an adaptation of *Henry VIII* (1911, dir. William Barker). The film was subject to a deal in which all prints had to be burned six weeks after the first screening and it seems shocking now that none survived to be rediscovered and repackaged for a contemporary audience. So far, so exclusive.

Absent in these two sons' childhoods and photographed as a professional in his adulthood, the ever-present Henry makes almost no showing in family photos that have filtered in her direction. His existence is verified through an imbrication of stills, programmes and promo shots, with immaculate makeup and flattering lighting, forever captured in a series of perfect poses. His status as 'picture postcard hero' means there exists a full deck of portraits and production postcards. Photography is the great disappearing act of endless reproducibility, an inexact science of corrosive chemistry. Henry Ainley is in disguise again. He's still incognito. He epitomizes the fiction of the veracity of photography, which stops subjects in their tracks using material already beginning to degrade. She built her story of Henry out of these fragments of representation gathered from disputable facts. It's the only way for her to know him.

Other representations of Henry and sources of information about him come from all over: books; those letters in the British Library Special Collections; recordings in the BBC audiotape archive; the British Film Institute (BFI) film archive; the Shakespeare Centre Library; the V&A Theatre Archives; the Mander & Michenson Collection; the Cartoon Archive; *Punch* magazine; the Royal Academy of Dramatic Art (of which he was president in 1931–33); the Royal Shakespeare Company; the National Portrait Gallery; and the Garrick Club archive.

Her dad's work is accessible from some of those same sources and appears on film, videotape and in books. She has seen three films in which he appears, although she has scanned the list often. Two of them, *As You Like It* and *I Dood It*, she owns as VHS copies (although she no longer has the domestic technology necessary to watch them), and the third, *The Agony and the Ecstasy*, she has watched on television. The BFI archive holds 22 of his films that can be viewed for the asking. He features in institutional histories about the Bristol Old Vic and Rose Bruford drama schools and in the books regularly published by his more famous old students from there.

Dr Who is the key to finding millions of versions of Ant. She can search across (on this day) 232,000,000 Dr Who fan websites. The BBC archive holds some tape and digital copies of the program and every UK bookshop has a Dr Who shelf. Libraries keep DVD box sets of the series and video and DVD copies of some of those other TV series and films he appeared in. She can also watch him on television occasionally since some kind of digital remastering of his character took place in the contemporary series of Dr Who. As a player Ant's existence is well documented, along with his father's and brother's; their insubstantiality as family members is accentuated by the number of sources of information about their professional selves. Their public representations make fictions of their existence. Their professional biographies have to stand in.

It's all there for the looking, apart from when it's not. Technology gives access and restricts it, by design or by accident. It has its limits. There are limits, for example, to the number of backups the BBC produces or the number of copies the V&A can keep or the speed of the program of digitization of the Newspaper Collection to make available those papers too delicate to touch. Only so many formats can be held at one time. Everything continues to exist forever on the internet: nothing gets lost, so they say. Innumerable items come to exist finally only as storage fodder. Then they are forever disappointing as catalogue items to the eager researcher because the fact that they are actually lost or otherwise unreachable is also a source of power, investing them with the value of the unattainable. So near, so far; so there, so gone. Choices have to be made with each new format about what can be transferred, about what will survive the transition with the ambient hiss and sizzle wiped clean or with the breadth of tone and color flattened. All nuance can be further diminished by the viewing apparatus, and what's lost in translation may in time be lost entirely. Archives revise their collections according to what extant technology allows researchers to play or see. Generally the consumer is only aware of what has been deemed worthy of transfer from analogue to digital, what's not considered too damaged or degraded to copy, from fix-corroded photograph to JPEG, by preferences and format incompatibility and corruption. Still, nothing can be captured, downloaded or stamped for keeps. Where the electronic connection is continually timed out, a holding image exists only as a marker of an absence that is always there, taunting, an intruder-alternative to what is sought.

The technology means that, pulped to its last copy, out of print and its paper pages acid-attacked, uncountable files of endless versions of this script will remain. Beyond that, life expectancy of access can be problematic. Stories persist in their longevity nonetheless; technologies often have shorter lives than secrets or memories, despite the promise of their manufacturers. The bait of limitless capacity in any and every successive new form of digital storage is a false promise held out to encourage early adoption by the user whose financial investment is crucial for a format to become embedded. The power of retrieval is enormous, yet it promises (the illusion of) an impossibility. The archive is forever a place of dreams and their disappointment. The archivist or researcher can retrieve only representations of artifacts of memory, and then only in a fragmentary form. That is what can be found at the archive: an evidence store, tagged and ordered, an itemization of clues, a documentary of the artifacts of the detection. It's what the detective fabricates out of what is uncovered at the archive that's important. She's engaging in the same kind of detective work that biographers of the reclusive and the uninterested are engaged in. She's a detective reconstituting traces left by others, rewriting the story. Refashioning the snippets and jigsaw pieces she finds fuels an appetite for more. This is all there is.

A 'distance value' is bestowed on the holdings of the archive by virtue of having to travel to an unknown destination; to develop new relationships with curators and managers; and then to wade through cataloguing systems and order material with which others are far more familiar. Since it takes trouble to get material from the archive, the past that it contains is packaged in a layer of accumulated promise of (in)completeness: scarcity *and* distance value. A visit to an archive is a performance dedicated to keeping at bay any prospect of conclusion, keeping arrival always deferred. Devoted to itself, the space has its own attractions of quietness, insulated from the outside by its own material, an atmosphere interrupted only by rustling paper and the click of drawers sliding shut, the low-voiced instruction from the keepers of the archive.

At the digital archive every search with a virtual embarkation point offers the flickering monitor, dynamic graphics, warning signals, instant response, electronic rather than mechanical sounds: searching in an online space for what may exist but can never be found. A fascination with the interface and the process of the search, and ambivalence over its object masks the fearful questioning: if I find it, what then? What's left? The process of always looking (because that thirst can never be slaked) and never finding is built into the system. She doesn't know what she's looking for and can't know and can't find it, since what she seeks is to find what's lost or broken or non-existent. The digital archive makes that process easily repeatable: to look again without the public embarrassment of obsession. For all its (pleasing) catalogues and systems, the archive remains (pleasingly) labyrinthine and impenetrable. While both the workaday and dream-like nature of the archive holds out that false assurance, in actuality what it offers is the mundane: the gap. How it is described is the main event, how it is told. That's the story. She's making something of it.

Aside from the deliberations of what to admit and what to exclude, archives can also play a part in the dissemination of false information. Not all the data can be relied upon and just because it's there doesn't mean you always want to know. The archive may not be able to guarantee the veracity of any information contained in its holdings, and it may not be the role of the institution to make pronouncements on the provenance and content of their holdings. It still seems surprising to come across misrepresentations presented as facts. The expectation remains that the archive is full of facts; make any use of what can be found there, sometimes it's wrong. It doesn't need to be made up.

She had always known that Henry had three wives, like her dad; and as far as she knew Henry had three mistresses too and a pair of children with each wife and each mistress. But she was a child making up symmetries for maximum impact and falsifying the mistress count in the process, exposing mistakes and misapprehensions of her own and others' too. She used to enjoy intoning this pattern to herself, she could believe that her life was governed by some of the same systems and rules gleaned from children's tales in which she took refuge. She was wrong about that just as she was wrong to imagine for the sake of poetic equivalence that father and son each had three wives. She found that out by reading it in print too: sleuthing in Ethel Hardie's book gave her the facts this time. The press was even more ill-informed than she was about this public figure. Henry's obituary in *The Times* mistakenly had it that he'd made 'several' films when the tally was more like 25 and he had been widely credited as one of the first English stage actors to move into film. *The Times,* among others, misinformed its readers about the number of Henry's children and who their mothers were. Her dad, tailoring-related recognition notwithstanding, was recognized in print as his father's only son (out of a cast of many). It's a slip of the public sphere. Perhaps it was an easy, if lazy, mistake to make when father and son both had a professional profile on the stage. Richard was also reported as one of only two children. The paper managed to get right the number of wives Henry had, but one of the women named was not his wife. Elsewhere Richard and his sister are attributed as children of Henry's wife, rather than their own mother, who went unmentioned. Keep up. *TV Times* miscast Antony too as Richard's son and Henry's grandson, slipping a generation in response to a reader's enquiry about the facial likeness between him and Henry. Another easy mistake to make.

Her own family archive lacks the distance value conferred on other archives but her storage methods mean she can go through the process of discovery over and over, so that she can always find something new when she looks again. Her refusal to categorize or even file in one place is a deliberate bid to extend this possibility. The impulse to keep separate piles can be traced back to a fear of losing the material: if it's not all in the same place, she won't be able to lose all of it. Although lacking the sense of place, in common with other archives hers provides its own style of validation while also always failing to deliver. The compulsion to return, to look again, is easily achieved. The constant promise, the continual disappointment, mirrors the double-edged nature of any archive. To know its contents too well, to be over-familiar, will wear it away, oxidize it into dust. Her acid breath will quicken the process of decay and the whole will expire, in all formats. The gaps won't be so visible, either. Like the unused space around the single image in the folder indexed under 'father, and self'.

Other people in the family have made deposits of a verbal, printed, audio and photographic type, some of a public nature and some private but she's the keeper. It's jobs for the girls. The keeper of this family archive is expected to write the definitive, minutely researched story of the acting Ainleys, the tale of a diminished dynasty, verified through long conversations and painstaking research. That's a work that is understood and sometimes even eagerly anticipated. Any half-decent detective could do it, deliver the goods, sign off and on to the next case, the next assembly of random to chase. As a detective she's as poor a specimen as she is a sister, and her motivations are open to question and suggestion. She's the archivist of family stories too, originally self-appointed and now tacitly recognized. She is the person who rips those stories apart too by delivering them up to public view where they stop belonging to the family. As if they ever did. She's also expected to know what a second cousin once removed is, and who they are. She can be relied upon to be curious enough to follow up on leads of 'new' family members and also to voice information about them that others in the family think is untrue. (They're right about that, even she can't be sure that she hasn't made it up).

Her dad used to make his own leads to follow too. He discovered and met his older brother Norman, the story goes, through his Family Yellow Pages habit of looking in local phone-books on any trips around the country to see if any Ainleys were listed. Norman was discovered in Eastbourne when they were on one of their holidays on the south coast. It's a habit she inherited from him to fill in the gaps but she doesn't seek them out wherever she goes like he did. She doesn't always want to know and she imagines he didn't either. She waits until she comes across them and then makes contact.

The contents of 2 Ennerdale Drive would have constituted an archive of 80 years in the life one family, settled and sedimented within its boundaries. There had been no history within the house other than this family's, with material from bills of sale and conveyancing documents to grocery bills and insurance certificates to postcards, and just maybe, a hoard of valuable Dr Who memorabilia. The house is itself the repository for the archive of this family. Nothing else has been allowed through the front door, and that's more than enough. It has contained the people and their documentation. No more future, it's run out of time. The house is empty of that family now, but full of promise still. It's an archive of the affect, of emotionally articulated space and ripe with documentation, such as it is.

Exhibit 5: A remarkable Hamlet

I'm on a mission for evidence, on the trail of the lost and forgotten. When I ask, nobody else in the family has ever seen this image or knew it existed. (What's she going on about now?) I held on to the expectation that this picture would turn up in some arcane dimension of the internet or in a mouse-damaged corner, a musty collection of a trading-broke antiquarian business or in a forgotten cousin's cupboard. The description of what I'm searching for develops into its own certificate of authenticity: it exists because I've decided it's from a production of *Hamlet*. It's a real piece of performance writing, a story for stage. It must be true. It must exist. The production details are verifiable. More details make it more true. For this train of thought to work, I only have to forget who it was who supplied the 'more details'.

Flashbackwards. My brothers and I stand around together at home, outside a cupboard we've turned into a sort of picture store. It's the early 1980s. We're snorting with laughter over a framed cartoon we've found of our grandfather. It's always been in our possession, carting our history around in boxes as we do, but we've only now got around to unwrapping it. We're not laughing with him. We're not kids anymore but it's still pleasing somehow to hoot and snigger at this picture of an old guy in tights with a ridiculously oversized head.

What a good laugh. It may be a measure of the effectiveness of the caricature that it would have offered a particular reading to the people who saw it when the play came out and it's still food for us to guffaw at. And 25 years after we were standing there it calls me, insists I find it. I have to find this picture because it's another image in the public realm, an artwork based on a play and a performance and a reputation. Despite everything I've said, I spend a lot of time looking and thinking

I'll find it. Looking becomes the work, the end in itself: it's the perfect diversion both from not finding and from writing.

It exists (still) because I've seen it. I discover that in this instance the dregs of memory can be wrung out to satisfy myself that this search has an object and a goal. I see an outsize, arrogant head on a strumpet body that disappears in a point like the genie effect on a Mac (the one I always turn off). And the body isn't so much clothed, it's more like it has been colored in, black felt-pen from the toes up, leggings to turtleneck or body stocking. The body is only important for its scale. Caricatures work when the subject has enough of a public profile within its scope of circulation to be recognizable in a distorted, exaggerated state, which then raises the profile further.

I'm tracking down the picture, the memory of a picture or a print trace on paper inscribed in my memory and now somehow vital because I've seen it in private and it existed in public. It's the (lack of) costume that somehow communicates Hamlet to me, so ahead of its time it looks in its minimalist effect. Knowing it relates to Hamlet will help pin it down, narrow the focus of the search. Or so I think. Henry first appeared in a productions of *Hamlet* at His Majesty's in 1910, ten years into his career, in a production by H Beerbohm Tree with an all-star cast including Ellen and Fred Terry along with Beerbohm Tree himself. Twenty years later he played the title role at the Haymarket Theatre in a Royal Command performance. At 50 this was certainly a late-career Hamlet and played by a man past his best work and well beyond personal acquaintance with the youthful moods and self-examination of the character. Whether this was Henry's finest hour or not, this must be the production that spawned the lost caricature since his role in the 1910 production was Laertes. He still gladdened the public eye enough to be at the center of a Royal Command performance and to be considered suitable to play the prevaricating Hamlet. That's my version. And there is a different story: the Hamlet suit is nothing but the artist's template with no connection to any particular production.

He's all image again then, he's endless pictures (and always the wrong one). I have to question the need to steel myself against a disappointment I'm so actively pursuing and the pursuit of which is causing me such enjoyment. Maintaining two developmental positions at once is an attempt to recognize the absence of the object and so the ability to do without it while incorporating it into a fantasy-search story. This causes me to feel excitement and anxiety, if not mourning or pain. In Judaism there are precepts surrounding the return of a lost object and how to undertake this, because it is considered a mitzvah, an act of human kindness and a fulfillment of commandment in the Torah, to return it properly. 'The object must be lost.' 'The owner must know he lost the object.' And so on. The caricature may not be the only lost object. I am not the owner, either, which would explain why I can't find it or return it.

Not a single specialist curator or librarian or bookseller has responded to me with a eureka moment, and said 'Ah yes, the Hamlet cartoon!' before deftly tracking it down in their system. 'Of course, I know it well, the Flaxman [or Spy or Furness or Bert Thomas] I believe!' as they mentally root through their collection, followed for me by the sound of cogs dropping into place. The pursuit spreads out into a series of apparently endless distractions of the online search. I characterize these as retrieval deficit or archive deficiency. This means it exists, they just haven't got it; it exists but I've given them the wrong search terms; it exists but the system is faulty. Email relationships are established with dedicated ranks of specialist keepers who pour forth suggestions, thumbnails, introductions and interest. Enthusiasm crackles back to me from most sources. The helpfulness (and efficiency) of strangers leads me through vaults of information, pinpointing close matches to my request, that are never quite close enough. This isn't going to work is it? The object isn't lost so much as discarded by us at a time when it was not thought to be worth keeping. The relationships end with professional regret.

A sheaf of disappointments has already been smothered by the next inquiry. Maybe this time, maybe this collection, this curator. In desperate circularity, I find myself searching in the same places, only realizing what I'm doing when the same search terms pop up in the field. Sometimes

I allow myself to think that a second go might throw up a different result, even from the same collection, with the same search terms.

So much stuff and none of it what I want. And it keeps arriving, more and more material that I don't want, that I've decided I don't need. I had no idea that there could ever be too much. The material is all more of the same, confirmation, public portraits, artifacts for public consumption. I'm sated with it, overfed, in fact. I'm sick of missing what I can't find, sick of finding what I don't want. Sick of finding more and more of what I'm not looking for and what I already (always) know. Somehow I'm not yet sick of looking. I think of the mountain of pictures, objects, books, furniture, papers, letters, diaries, jewelry, ornaments, clothes, knives, photographs, glasses from the house where the picture store was that has been divided up, disposed of or just plain disappeared. The caricature is just more stuff that's been junked. Getting rid of it is an appeasing sacrifice, to purge the memory, to lift the weight, or is it lack of interest, plain tiredness? I think of suffocation and of loss, as though it's this stuff that is the remains of people. The conversation isn't over; I've lost the possibility of saying 'this is it, this is the one, this is me'. Symbolically, the absence of the caricature is equally meaningful as its presence would be.

Several avenues of inquiry bring up a definite no: The Garrick Club, the British Library Print Room, Offstage Books, National Portrait Gallery (Heinz Collection), David Drummond at Pleasure of Past Times in Cecil Court. I come to see this certainty, long after the pin-prick of disappointment has faded, as a bonus and an impetus to fuel me on to the next venue. Travelling on and on, in time if not in space, keeps arrival at bay, keeps me safe. The archivists and proprietors I approach know they haven't got that (which I want) but what about this (which they have)? With each admission of defeat comes a note enclosing a suggestion: 'You might try ...' and a list of related holdings – photographs or figurines, say. (It's a reproach: why can't you want all this that we have got?) Often I already have tried that avenue of enquiry, yet I'm diverted to look again at what they do have, to avoid wondering whether what I'm looking for exists at all, or if that matters anyway. There's always somewhere else to try until you yourself call a halt.

Punch archive promised 'about a dozen' cartoon references and one of them surely had to be the one. There was a build-up of expectation waiting for them to arrive by email as low-res JPEGs. Each one is opened with quickly dampened excitement. They are mainly cartoons rather than caricatures. I'm getting to the point where I have to force myself to open attachments. I know I'm reaching the end. Dutifully, ungratefully, I print them all out.

The biggest disappointments follow the longest trails. Staff at the V&A Theatre Archive suggested I might find what I was looking for in a feature in *Titbits* as a possibility, for a reproduction of the caricature. Although only a possibility. They've met me and my kind before, they know they must not raise hopes in the searcher. I really wanted it to be *Titbits*, a magazine with a silly name, the *Heat* of its day. It would have been so right for a teasing caricature of a heartthrob of his times. I decided *Titbits* must have been part of the joke, part of our amusement when we were looking through the cupboard. The magazine might even have still existed at that point, a prurient little publication that had lost its way and become outdated.

When I visit the V&A Theatre Archive it's one of the first images I see from my order. The page from *Titbits* has two illustrations; and one of them is a caricature of Mr Henry Ainley. It is in the style of the image I'm imagining but it's not the one. It's a caricature as 'himself' rather than as Hamlet. The picture caption gives no credit, it reads only *Mr Henry Ainley, seen by a caricaturist*, so no clues there. The piece was one of a series of 'A Great Actor's Life Story: What Shaw had to say about My Malvolio', first of a two-parter, from 23 November 1929. Henry gets the byline: it's twice removed then, ghost-ghost written. The other image is a headshot of George Bernard Shaw which is almost the same size as the drawing of Henry's entire body. Teasingly (what else did I expect from *Titbits*?) Henry tells us that Shaw said his performance of Malvolio in *Twelfth Night* was so 'dismal and melancholy' that he would make a 'remarkable Hamlet'. This is less than six months before he plays the role at the Haymarket, a performance that one critic eulogizes as 'the infinite variety of Henry Ainley's Hamlet', so Shaw is probably guilty here of trailing a production that had already been planned but not yet announced.

The files are delivered by archivists to the Reading Room manager who brings each one to me separately, drip-feeding. I fear ordering up too much material in case I won't get through it or not ordering enough so that I won't find anything to absorb my disappointment. Next up, an album of around 40 publicity portrait postcards arrives at my allotted table. Many of them are credited to 'Sasha of Hart Street, WC1', some have details of a production printed on the back. I see likenesses in the album pages of the other men of my family who appear on the stage too, and some who don't. I see how certain looks skip generations but how they are clearly caught in another image. The cards are sleeved in pristine cellophane sheaths that look untouched by any grubby-fingered researcher since a be-gloved archivist slid them into the individual pockets. Some have a metalized sheen to them; a set for *Faust* has been subjected to a ghastly, ghostly hand-tint. Some have a look of solarization, with a surface showing the virtues of positive and negative. One is a novelty postcard shaped like a playing card, with a cut-out of two ancient columns between which stands Henry as Mark Anthony in *Julius Caesar* (at the St James's in Duke Street). The overdose-induced befuddlement of quantity goes some way to allow an optimistic gloss to hang over this visit and every other time. I can only find what isn't here, but … this is the right subject, the right style, the right character, the right media. I could almost convince myself it means I'm getting closer. As though I'm following a trail and it has the capacity to get hotter.

I am condemned to keep looking for, and finding, what isn't there. The sources are not endless though, any more than my appetite. They appear as a spiral of possibilities that briefly widens and just as quickly tightens up, shutting me out. My options are limited and it's a choice to keep looking. The location of the institutions follows a similar spiral form outwards from a hub in central London, in the heart of the West

End theater district. The locations, when the visits are to physical rather than virtual spaces, cluster around the West End in London, the proper place for anything theater-related, from the Garrick Club and RADA archives, the offices of *The Stage* and specialist bookshops like Offstage.

One of those family members who adds copiously to the archive says he has a 1905 caricature of Henry by Harry Furniss. A prickle of expectation is over almost before it starts. It's the same one that I have seen on the National Portrait Gallery website, with the stare and wild hair and the doughy look he grows into (or towards which he's always had a tendency). The look of a Yorkshireman, some might say. The scaling of the caricature, the outsize head again in profile, gives him the look of a goblin perched on the end of a sofa, looking over the arm, with one leg folded beneath him like a girl. A crest of hair like a fin mirror-images previously unnoticed facial features of crooked beaky nose and pointed witchy chin. With little sharp-toed shoes and a long coat this doesn't add up to an image of gravitas. In the printout from the Portrait Gallery I read the image is classified under 'in profile', 'lounging portraits' and 'prominent men'.

I'm not sure what I have lost, or why I imagine anything is lost other than expectation and possibility. This would be equally the outcome of finding it, or it could bring a liberation from the need to search. While there's an object of desire, I'm not lost. I get something out of this. Laura Marks calls the object that activates this process at once a pacifier (there is something) and an unbearable reminder (it's not the right something). Ultimately it can only ever be an unbearable reminder of loss, signifying something missing and missed. I am making the choice. I'm not the owner of the *Titbits* page either, which I would have judged an adequate substitute for the caricature. To place an order for a copy of the page at the V&A I have to first ascertain copyright and request permission from the copyright holder to reproduce it. Copyright rests with the holder of Henry Ainley's estate, and I attempt to discover whom this is by ordering a copy of the will.

There is no will. And here we go again. Or rather, here we don't go again. There is no will because either the death was recent, the estate value was below the probate threshold, or the estate transferred to a surviving spouse. I set my heart on that image, that's clear. Once I start to wonder why, wonder what I have buried there, I know exactly. It's the three of us, my brothers and I, in a brief and occasional moment when we're laughing together, over the idea that the man in the picture is said to be our grandfather.

She might not recognize his signature but he looks familiar enough in pictures given the number of his descendants who share his looks, the similarities clear in his postcard portraits. Enough visual resemblance is running through them then but she finds his voice, or its indexical trace on audiotape, unrecognizable. As she hears it, it's a reminder of their intercultural, intergenerational displacement. Henry the actor was famed as much for his voice on stage as for his looks: 'His magnificent elocution' was used to make early acoustic recordings in 1899 by the Gramophone Company when the technology and industry were in their infancy. He was in at the beginning of commercial sound recording. In 1908 a recording of his voice was used to introduce the trademark of His Masters Voice and later, when the company had become known as HMV, he made trial electric recordings for them.

His culture of theater is not hers, his class is not hers either, and he doesn't sound how she thinks granddads should sound, even allowing for the fashionable oratorically exaggerated performance style that 'actors were expected to be more "vocal" in those days'. That's what her dad wrote to a Mrs Brenda Niccol of Emm Plains, New South Sales in Australia, who contacted him about her mother meeting Henry before the First World War. Richard wrote that Henry's first wife 'Miss Bess Peacock' had encouraged him to join the amateur theater group and helped him with voice production. But how would she know how granddads sound? He's not the only one in the family with actorly vocalization: her dad's was described as a 'resonant and musical voice' (James Agate, *Sunday Times*); and Ant's 'cat-like purr and malevolent chuckle' as The Master were prized (Tony Hadoke, *The Guardian*). She's used to others in the family being able to do things with their voice, change it, use it to make people laugh. With Henry, though, she has heard nothing except his performance. Maybe there was nothing else to hear, both his reported and imagined persona suggest that there was never a time when he was off-duty. For her all-but-imaginary and ever-present grandfather, there's no distinction between the performative and the private voice. The so-called performative is real, the standard; it's all a stage whether it's the home front or West End or provincial playhouse.

Henry only just crossed over into the talking pictures; a man prized for his voice was somehow robbed of it through the technology not being in place at the time. All but two of Henry's films were silent movies. *The First Mrs Fraser* (he'd already starred in the stage version) was his only other talkie apart from *As You Like It*. For more than 20 films, in a substantial part of his career then and in his personal life he's a presence without a voice, a speechless man with only a printed script. As she tries to find connection Henry's oratory alienates her in content, form and delivery. Silent or declaiming, he's a disembodied unknown voice. He's the man without a voice (she doesn't know what he sounds like); the man-as-voice famed for his voice onstage ('his famous organ voice', his voice 'to fill a great cathedral with music worthy of its stones'; the silent man (star of pre-sound films); the unknown voice man (star of another age); the man with voice as instrument, his speech musical, mellifluous. His is the voice separated from its source, except onstage.

Voiceless for her, who never heard him talk except for speaking lines captured on magnetic tape or relayed through celluloid, he is disconnected from his own voice, professional and personal. There's little access to his voice for her or for anyone else now. She can't hear it: she has no memory and not much tape but she does have an audio cassette recording from the BBC archive via her sister, of Henry reading Tennyson's 'The Charge of the Light Brigade' (1854). He made this recording for the Gramophone Company who gave out the information that Tennyson was his favorite poet and 'The Charge of the Light Brigade' his favorite poem.

Rolling his rs, well, theatrically, like a tiger's purr, the style of his delivery makes it hard for her to understand the words. The rhythm whips along, he's practically singing, trilling the sounds of the words. The unfamiliar 1920s pronunciation and cadence becomes almost foreign. She recognized the poem as famous but couldn't identify it. The words that she can't catch become irrelevant because the emotion they carry is communicated to her as though it is music. The old-fashioned sentiments jangle horribly. At the end of the recording he almost shouts the line 'God save the King' in a 'Cry "god for Harry! England and St George"' voice (*Henry V*, IIIi31).

Through following the trail of Henry and his voice, in pursuit of her own, like his, absent and present, loud and silenced, she finds something of it, recovers what was probably already (and always) there. Through using his unfamiliar voice she's getting back to her own sounding familiar again. His is an embodiment of voice that she can only hear second-hand at most. An unfamiliar public voice highlights the absence of the familiar private one. With little enough shared ground between them, they are both disconnected from their voices. They share the acousmatic voice, one that is removed from its source and technology lets both of them down.

She never met Henry to hear him speak in a private, domestic setting or to call him Harry as intimates and family did. It would be the act of an imposter and only serve as a reminder that she never knew him. It would be a false claim of closeness. Making bloodless family relationships is one thing but she shies away from the presumption of pretending to familial intimacy. Within

the gradations of intimacy theirs is one of blood only, not famil-
iality or familiarity. It may be her family but in so many ways it's
her story only as its author, not as family member. She's allowed
to hold it for a short time on that basis and deposit her version
but only until it's written over again.

Their past becomes her plaything as long as she acknowledges
that she is also in its grasp. It's something of a loan, an illusion of
a loan even. There's an element of displacement too in her lack of
recognition. Probably if she had known Henry he would have
been like generic grandfather writ large: ancient, kindly, distant,
generous, cantankerous, affectionate, impossible. He would have
had a lot to say and a lot to hide, to keep to himself. Just like the
parents in fact, only more so.

This is what can be found. It's a trail of her own making that
she has resurfaced. She's a detective of the paper trail and this is
what she has found, uncovering print and buildings in her wake.
Remembering what never happened, making up what did with a
jumble of maps with routes and journeys and dreams and parties
and fictions. A trail of temporariness, ordered just so for now.
This will do. This is as good as it gets. She has found this much
and put together a case for its own defense and prosecution. To
detect is to find, to notice, to uncover, to locate, to scent. The
investigator makes an investment. This is the detritus, a towering
block of paper that has arisen out of the rubble of family and
scraps of stories. It's a viable construction, whether intermittently
or regularly sustainable or sustaining.

These are her findings, if you want to call them that. If you
want to call her detective, that's up to you now. There's something
to be said for not finding what you're looking for; for finding
what you're not looking for, the always-already. Looking has to
mean not knowing, never knowing what it is you're looking for
and always finding something that you didn't know you wanted.
You might not want it, but you did start looking and this is what
you get. You have to keep looking, keep going in case you get

there. And there's something to be said too for accepting the findings of the not knowing, for using what's there, what turns up. It's all found information, the difference comes in how it's categorized, what you decide you want to believe, what you don't believe but what can be used just as well. It can be ignored, or it can be lost again, to await an uncovering at another juncture, to be re-embraced for another story.

Chapter 4

Always never there

Henry played Orlando, the male lead in *As You Like It*, in one of his earliest stage roles in a production at the Scala Theatre in Tottenham Street. Thirty years later he played the part of the exiled Duke in the film version with Laurence Olivier as Orlando, along with his son Richard. From a family point of view, father and son having acting roles in the same film is big. For Richard it's an early-career moment while for Henry it's at the tail end of a full stage career and another item on a long list of film credits. It's the son's first film and the father's last and the second of the two talkies he acted in. Henry had already filmed in Hollywood; his son was set to soon to follow the example. *As You Like It* may not be an outstanding example of Shakespeare on film but it is Britain's first Shakespeare sound feature and Olivier's earliest Shakespeare performance on film. Henry was having or was shortly to begin his affair with Laurence Olivier. Henry's career is coming to an end, Olivier is coming into his own. Another succession is being effected, and not only that between father and son. Privately and professionally then, this is weighty for the three of them.

As You Like It is a romantic comedy, a tale of exile and return and withdrawal and acknowledgement of family ties. Most of the action takes place in the Forest of Arden. Arden is both Shakespeare's mother's maiden name and the name of an area that is forever 'Shakespeare country' in the Midlands county of Warwickshire, the location of his birthplace, Stratford upon Avon. The youthful shepherd Sylvius, played by son Richard, belongs in the arcadian forest; father Henry has been exiled there from the palace in the city, usurped by his younger brother and sets up an alternative court of outsiders in the forest. It's the Duke's band of wise, saddened merry men who set the scene for the transformative powers of the forest. Here is a welcome unknown outside its leafy glades; the welcome is extended to strangers too, who have five acts to realize what this place can give them, indeed before they can realize it.

The forest is enormously bucolic as places of exile go. It is a refuge that's alive with romantic possibility, a place where disguise and mistaken identity are magically uncovered to bring happy results as secrets emerge. This topsy-turvy place is one where, unbound from the strictures of convention, unusual answers can emerge to questions about the suitability of love objects; the intricacies of family relationships; and whose opinions merit attention. Fantastic events unfold with series of coincidences, complicated family connections and parallel plots, which together will provide a neat resolution.

Sylvius and Phebe, shepherd and shepherdess, provide a comic subplot of rustic revelry to the main action between Orlando and Rosalind, daughter of the exiled Duke. Phebe will come to value and happily embrace the love that bashful Sylvius is offering while Rosalind and Orlando will be reunited. Rosalind has been banished from the court because Orlando, the younger and less favored son of Sir Rowland de Boys, has fallen in love with her and she is considered an unworthy match even for a second son. Orlando has run away from persecution by his big brother and his father's favorite, Oliver. They may be thwarted in their love but they are destined to be joined together again by the end of the play. Rosalind is disguised as the boy Ganymede in the forest, where her beloved Orlando fails to recognize her and posts 'Wanted' notices on trees all around the forest. Have you seen her? No, but then nor has he.

So they're going, her and her brothers, on an outing to what was then called the National Film Theatre on the South Bank in London to watch this family home movie and double first of

British cinema. The program notes say that the screening was part of a retrospective season of Olivier films. He was still alive then, the early 1980s, so the season may have been promoted to mark an anniversary of some sort, 60 years on the stage maybe. They don't want to seem too excited or proud or anything like that. It's only a bit of fun. It's embarrassing, really. Seeing your dad on celluloid in his youth is shocking. He looks like someone else, as everyone's dad does before their children were born. Did he really exist before I did? Isn't being my dad what he's for? He's picked up an American accent so he sounds like an American doing a 1930s English accent for Shakespeare. And then there's seeing your grandfather onscreen in the same film, whom none of them met. It's the magic of the movies and then some, in neon. They have to take it in their stride, even though they've never seen the film with the two of them in it before, never seen their dad looking so young, never seen him move in his prewar, pre-disability stride. To talk about how weighty it is for these three would be to recognize the enormity of what they've never seen, of what and how much was lost. They'd have to acknowledge that they missed something and they all know not to do that, individually or as a group.

This first time she saw the film, she almost missed her dad, uncertain that could really be him. Then she's entirely blown away, her guts and blood and brain cells are all over the plush seats. She can't understand why no one else is reacting. It's him! How can that beautiful, simple, lanky boy be her dad? And how can that Phebe be so foolish as to spend the whole film spurning his adoration? What does Phebe think she's doing, holding out on her dad? She's sold already, in an anguished non-com romance that's no less potent for its object being dead and on celluloid and her dad. It's the moving-ness of the image that does for her, its illusion of unflattened three-dimensionality and his voice moves her, even though it sounds very different from the voice she thinks she remembers. She can see he was alive in a way that a film still or photograph doesn't suggest. The film gives her back something she never had. He made this film 20-odd years before she arrived, though he was already a father then. The Sis, his eldest child, is here too and she doesn't notice the eruption. It's only a film. She's seen it before.

This public screening could have been a genuinely private family event. They learn for the first time on this evening that as family members they can request screenings of productions featuring relatives that are held in the national archive. The film is a like a fossil, petrified many times over, from several angles, starting with a material trace of a play performance. It's a filmic representation of stories they know already, that everyone knows already, with its themes of recognition, legitimacy, disrupted family narrative and thwarted love. They can see themselves, or at least their ancestors, written in. And they can see them onscreen too.

Fastforward 25 years to a viewing in her sitting room of a rough VHS copy of a bad print of the same film and she realizes how little her dad appears onscreen. She knows that Sylvius is only a small part, but knowing it doesn't quite make it add up. She's noting down his entrances so that she can rewind and pause to make close study of this man who is billed under the same name as her father. Twenty-five years haven't stopped it being thrilling. She's tempted to make screenshots so that she can look them into existence until the paper wears away and the poor print disintegrates into a kind of organic pixelation. At her touch he will be incorporated via her fingerprints and he'll always be there. All his files will copy over on to her operating system so that she will be able to access all of him whenever she wants to. She will be able to distill him out and make him tall again. She will never again forget what he sounds like. It's unbelievable what technology can do.

After repeated viewings of the film Henry's mellifluous voice is becoming recognizable, a rich trace of her granddad, although it still divides them in time and space. His audio performance of the past in the present sounded as alien as covered furniture legs initially and is warming gradually to a familiarity. I'm finding him, I'm getting there. Full and vibrant, his is a voice perfectly attuned to that old-fashioned style of Shakespearian production. It's funny, snigger, and there's an enjoyable visceral thrill. That boom! That depth!

Magical endings may be standard for the stories involved here but it doesn't quite happen for her in this filmic version of the Ainley boys. In a theater production Sylvius and the old Duke would have been on stage at the same time. The gangly shepherd (in a suit, she hopes, of Lincoln green) can teach the young nobleman Orlando a thing or two about finding the way to a woman's heart. Sylvius and Phebe aren't so foolish after all, with their not-so-comic parallel plot. She scanned the film avidly in pursuit of a frame where both Henry and Richard appear. At first (re-)viewing she thinks she's found it, in the 'recognition' scene, fittingly enough, in Act 5 when it all comes together. Sylvius isn't there, but then a shepherd would not appear in the foreground of a final tightly cropped tableau scene of recognition so she rewinds the jumpy VHS copy repeatedly and peers again at the gathering. If one photograph exists of the two brothers, and one of the father and daughter, there must be one shot available at least of father and son, surely. Even a still would have enough depth. She can let herself be convinced by a photograph. What she wants must be for them both to jump script, if only for long enough for her to see them together, in order to stamp her recognition of the celluloid statement of their relationship.

gathering of Ainleys at Rule's Restaurant. At the far end of the table is Anthony, youngest son of the late Henry Ainley; on his right his half-brother Richard. The girl in glasses on the right of the picture is Pokoe, Richard's daughter. Son: Two more Ainleys.

ting out on their own acting careers.
Anthony is just back from acting Shakespeare in Arizona. 'They lived in

Exhibit 6: A Gathering of Ainleys

We are seated along both sides of a narrow restaurant table set for a party. Several tables have been strung together for the occasion in one corner of the restaurant, or maybe in one of the private rooms that Rules keeps precisely for this kind of party. The walls of these rooms in Covent Garden are heavy with pictures hung randomly and crookedly. The pictures are doubtless of a theatrical nature, of characters played and productions raised by the characters who famously make up a significant portion of Rules' clientele, who use the place as an 'unofficial "greenroom" for the world of entertainment from Henry Irving to Laurence Olivier'.

One of several absences recalled in this photograph is my memory of this dinner: it's unlikely that I can remember it, and only partly because I am four years old in the picture. My version is probably no more than a memory of someone else's story of the dinner. It doesn't belong to me. This report of the dinner in a newspaper is both part of the event and a prompt for it. I don't remember any real facts about this party, other than I can see that I was there when it happened. Even that is open to interpretation, apparently.

The party is being held in honor of The Sis and our uncle Ant, to highlight their careers. She maintains doggedly that I was not there and it was her party, so she should know but in the picture I am next to her at the table. Perhaps she wanted to sit beside someone other than her grubby little sister or maybe I spilt something on her clothes. She says I'm thinking of another party. Either way I'm missing from her picture, even if I'm there. There are other absences. My mum is not visible, but I can pretend that's her handbag I recognize and that might be her glass of wine parked in the place opposite my eldest brother, who looks the real bar mitzvah boy here, although he never was. Had my mum been sitting in what looks like it could have been her place, the photographer's view of my sister, the party girl, would have been blocked. The table continues beyond the frame, so whoever was sitting there is missing too. I can't be sure who that might have been and not knowing makes them doubly absent, but I can think of at least two more family members and a few friends whom I would have expected to be invited.

Our party needed a longer or differently shaped table or the photographer a different lens to accommodate the whole party. Even that wouldn't have been enough to complete the picture. The last and biggest missing is Henry Ainley, father of the party's host, my dad Richard, and one of its honored guests, Antony. Except Henry isn't missing either. He creeps into the picture caption; he manages almost to take over the role of host. Henry is present even in the choice of Rules, where 'the history of the English stage adorns the walls' in London's oldest restaurant and purveyors of culinary classics, these days contemporized. The newspaper column is titled 'Two more Ainleys' and it's the longest piece on the page. The column gives more information about Henry than anyone else present except my sister. So which two Ainleys is the headline writer talking about, again? The reader is told about Henry's family nickname (and my sister's), about the nationality of his wives, about the accoutrements of his fame (and hers, incipient). Henry plays the king, he is the king. He is forever the standard by which his sons are recognizable, even so long after his death. Without Henry there's no story. Voiceless, he hovers over the party and every other occasion, landing on the page.

I went to Rules for another theatrical occasion, years after this picture was taken. I would say that I ate grilled Dover sole both times but it's only the idea of the food that lingers and it's not on the menu anymore, if it ever was. That time it wasn't Henry who hovered over the evening but Richard, and I was the ill-at-ease, always over-shadowed child.

The journalist clearly has some trouble with the web of relation-ships in this rather tangled family. Most of the space in the column and in the picture caption is taken up with descriptions of family connection: youngest son and half-brother and uncle and niece as if he's counting it out on his fingers, trying to make some sense of it all by repeating it to himself. I know how he feels. He calls himself the odd man out, and says he found it 'delightful but a little confusing'.

On the table I can see side plates; seven wine glasses; two stem half-pint glasses of the type then used for squash or bottled beer; a floral table decoration; and my sister's napkin still sculpted, sitting in front of her. A lemon quarter on my brother's sideplate is a hint that there may be smoked salmon, brown bread triangles and butter curls, but I'm making stereotypical menu-guesses.

The younger members of the party are seated in the foreground of the image, their automatic grins turned on at the photographer's request to look at the camera. My eldest brother, seal-like and bursting out of his skin, is closest to the camera. Middle brother peeks over eldest brother's head, a miniature version two places down. Both of them have crewcuts. On the other side of the table I'm sporting a white Bri-nylon knitted hairband which matches the enormous napkin that's tied around my neck, presumably a preventative measure and a clue to why my sister might have decided to wipe from her memory my presence at her side and even at the table.

I'm looking at a photocopy of a newspaper page so here on the page in this form it's a coarse-screen newsprint halftone of an original photograph, xerographically reproduced, now digitally screened and slightly enhanced, and printed electronically. I'm removed from it several times over already. The coarseness of the dot of the halftone, coupled with the darkening wrought by the copying process used on a yellowing press cutting means it's a difficult image to read. The image appeared in the Londoners' Diary in the *Evening Standard* (Saturday 11 April 1964).

It's a portrait of family, or some of it. Four people in the picture are unidentified by the diarist and I'm not going to mention them either. They're not forgotten. Of the ten people in the picture, half are still alive. It's a private family party played out in public. It's the public family at private performance. It's the photograph of a party to publicize the careers of the young Ainley actors, while focusing heavily on the founding member of what must have seemed a rooted-enough dynasty at that time to have its family parties deemed of passing interest to other Londoners. It's the theater of the domestic and the public stage, all at once, exposing the private occasion, folded over and over, into itself, inside out. We're making a spectacle of ourselves.

While Henry was absent but never far distant in representation, very few pictures of her grandmother survive in the family archive. She was a glamorous, wealthy American (Irish-American, according to the National Portrait Gallery in London although James Riddle, her great-grandfather left County Donegal in 1772). She was married suitably into European nobility and then divorced out of it, which wasn't the desired outcome. No longer wealthy (still credit rich, maybe), she built a new bohemian life as a prolific popular novelist and became the mistress of a prominent figure in the English theater and mother to two of his children.

She died at the age of 82 in 1957, some 50 years after William Nicholson drew her portrait in 1907 or thereabouts which was used as an author's portrait. Reproduced in some of her books, it's a fragment of Nicholson's drawing, a portrait of a dark-haired woman in her middle years with the poise of an adult woman past her early glow. What she was is easy enough to define; there's some way to go to find out who she was. Even working out what to call her is elusive and that's probably just how the Baroness played it, how she wanted it. She had some weight to throw around, even as a woman of her day. She certainly made some choices.

Always hearing her grandmother referred to as Bijou, before learning her full name, the granddaughter thought that was her real name. It was a nickname, it turned out, and one of several. When she learned that her dad used Riddle as a stage name early in his career, she had always thought it was an attempt at enigmatic humor rather than a name to which he had some claim. Riddle was Bijou's maiden name, and for him was suitably anonymous unlike his dad's second name. Granddaughter uncovered yet another name for the Baroness-to-be: Huzzard, which was her second name. After her marriage, her full name was Bettina Riddle Freifrau von Hutten Zum Stolzenberg so Baroness von Hutten, which she took as her penname, seems almost restrained compared to the extravagances that might have crowded the covers of her books.

She didn't remember her dad talking much about his mother except about their peripatetic lifestyle. She had always known that her dad had never been to school, although he could speak five languages. This facility with languages was to secure him the post in the US Third Army as interrogator in Belgium, Germany and Italy in the Second World War and later allowed him to recite verse in the original in his one-man shows. For a long time, fuelled by romanticized children's books, she thought his family had been too poor to send him to school. When she knew more about his life, she realized that his schooling years were largely spent accompanying his mother on something not unlike the Grand Tour of Europe. 'Family fortunes fluctuated', he wrote in a publicity leaflet for his oratorical shows, graced by an Angus McBean promo portrait. The family moved not just around Europe but up and down the social scale as circumstances dictated. The Baroness travelled as (sub)society ladies with absurd nicknames did: extensively, stylishly and for long periods, taking in the usual cultural stopping places in France, Italy and Monte Carlo. Already familiar with Germany, she may have been keen to revisit Dresden, Heidelberg and Berlin before passing through Flanders and Holland and back to Dover.

At about the same time as the Baroness was roaming the continent and behaving badly and trading on her name, the story goes, Great-Aunt Ennerdale Drive might have been making her way across some of the same ground. For her, the inevitable adjective of intrepid has to attach to lady traveler. Of more slender but perhaps also less variable means than her not-yet relation by not-marriage, the difference in their resources may have matched the difference in their experience. When each of them returned to England, one arrived to a ready welcome in a suburban semi and one to a less certain but probably more central destination. 'Unaccompanied' travel was considered a more suitable pastime for society ladies, well-heeled lady anthropologists or philanthropists, all with retinues or companions, than for other women. The aunties were not ladies, and not women either by some accounts, if not wives or mothers. They find roles for themselves nonetheless, in Colindale and around the world, travelling and providing shelter for others, making family.

Like the confusion about her grandmother's name, the only stories she heard as a child about the Baroness didn't make any sense to her; like how she converted to Catholicism at the tail end of a fairly scandalous and unreligious life so that she could be nursed by nuns in an inclement old age. Eventually she got the gist. The Baroness was opportunistic, pragmatic, unreliable and a right character, she had to say. She wouldn't recognize her by voice either, not even by face. Her elder brother, who met the Baroness at least once, said that she was of the 'here's a sixpence, little boy, now run away and play' school of relative. She's not convinced that the woman ever really existed beyond the gold-foil-blocked spines of her novels.

The Baroness's series of best-selling novels featured the eponymous Pam, who fitted perfectly into a teenager's pantheon of romantic heroines: winning, sensitive, unconventional, rootless, principled, intelligent, headstrong, tragic, unlucky in love but adored ... There would be tears but it would all come out in the wash for this independent and spirited but finally loved creature. (But certainly not by the end of the first book in the series).

In her preface to *Pam*, the author writes 'So, gibbet my literary inabilities, laugh at my literary follies, weep over my literary dullness, but impute not to me the views of my characters.' It's worse than that. She's more of a character than a person: she *is* her character. She *is* Pam. It's the only way to know her grandmother through her scripted life-into-novel form. Fiction is life. It's Pam who's the figure in her life who comes closest to being a grandmother. Her existence as a paper-only character is no disqualification. Pam is her grandmother or her grandmother is Pam or Bijou or both, knowable to her only through, only as, fiction. And although she was clear that the position of Pam is already taken, that didn't stop her wanting to be Pam too.

Fiction was a lifeline for the Baroness, she needed the money and discovered a gift. Pam-in-the-book writes too. She keeps journals as a young girl and stories for magazines when she is reduced to living in a rented room on the wrong side of town (oh horror) with her wagelessly devoted maidservant Pilgrim. In a strangely realistic twist, Pam doesn't come close to making a living out of her stories, unlike her creator. *Pam* was hugely popular. She clearly wasn't the only reader for whom *Pam* hit the spot, it was more than grand-daughterly loyalty. Her copy of this 'round, unvarnished tale' is a reprint dated September 1928, and a staggering 550,000 in total were printed of this edition. A print run of half a million more than 20 years after publication of the first edition in 1905 would suggest that the author needn't have worried about critical response or assumptions about the extent of autobiographical content. Bijou kept good publishing company too. Her fellow authors in the series included Leo Tolstoy, Margaret Kennedy and Rider Haggard. *What Became of Pam* (1906, with five further impressions; new edition in 1910 with 13 impressions), another sequel appeared in an edition by Heinemann who also published Jack London and HG Wells.

She knew Pam in words, now she wanted to see how she looked. She needed *Pam* illustrated. Seeing her on the page would propel her through a slightly distorted range of chimerical mechanisms of recognition and curiosity than those that would snap into place on seeing an image of anyone she's interested in, distantly, or even people in production stills. She tracked down a version of *Pam* with pictures, investing in two sequels as well. *Pam at Fifty* looks for a resolution to a story that begins at the end of childhood. The book is dedicated to one Thaddeus, which is the name of Pam's favorite son in the novel: maybe *Pam* also took pleasure in muddying the imagined and the real. She hoped that *Pam's Own Story* would extend and illuminate new perspectives on the nature of narrative, as a first-person rewrite of the original. Instead it was close to a straight transposition of reported speech into direct dialogue and any shift in commentary is negligible. By the time she'd ploughed through them she knew enough about Pam, young and not so young, in first- and third-person voice.

Pam with pictures took six weeks of surface mail to arrive. Presumably it came by ocean liner just as Baroness von Hutten might have crossed the pond in during her dollar princess years, in furs and sustained by a cocktail or two, or in her dotage attended by a bevy of medicinal nuns. The name Bettina was on the cover, her 'real' name. Who on earth is that? Any of her other books are credited to Baroness or even The Baroness von Hutten. It's startling because she was never known by the name Bettina to the family on the UK side of the Atlantic. She was a woman for whom everyone had a different name, in fiction and in life, a woman not to be pinned down. And that's permission enough to call her another person entirely. To see Bettina is strange, yes, because she's really called, might as well be called, Pam.

Published in 1905 by AL Burt Company in New York, there are four plates in the book, one is a frontispiece. All the illustrations are signed by B Martin Justice. Each of them depicts a pivotal scene in the narrative: Pam in her Arcadia with the man who is to be her lifelong and unattainable paramour; the illegitimate Pam leaving the social safety of her grandfather's house, following a characteristically unacceptable impulse; Pam spurning a suitor, compromised by the man she cannot have; and Pam in society, but with no indication of what society or at what cost. The pictures do the job well enough, of catching the light and setting the scene. The facial features look as if they have been reinscribed with a heavier, thicker mark before the printing process, so overdone are they. A piece of the text accompanies each of the pictures as a caption. There's 'Arcadia'; 'You know the results of disobeying that command'; 'And you would have to say about it – exactly nothing'; and, delightfully, 'The monkey in her arms a curious addition to the picture she made'. Any number of readings is possible, within and outside the story in the novel.

Each of the four images also has a stamp-sized line drawing at the bottom right-hand corner of the page, as a prophetic comment on the picture that it punctuates, a representation to suggest what comes after. An image of two outsize butterflies sets off 'Arcadia': indicating a utopia for two only perhaps, while others risk a more fragile affair of bliss and danger. Fluttering through the bougainvillea that proliferates in that landscape, setting down briefly to collect and distribute pollen, inhabitants here lead a charmed and precarious existence. In 'You know the results of disobeying that command' disobedient Pam faces a closed door. She stands next to an older woman with a different kind of hat, her servant, (Jane) Pilgrim who is her other constant companion aside from Caliban, a pet monkey, which she holds in her arms. Their luggage sits behind them. In 'And you would have to say about it – exactly nothing' a lone figure departs, eyes downward. 'Spurned' is branded into those lines. This is a retreat from unrequited love. The incongruous line, 'The monkey in her arms a curious addition to the picture she made' captions a stamp-sized cherub struggling to get free from a nest of brambles, the barbed snares of lurve.

• • •

A heavy cloud is forming of everything that's left unspoken and unrepresented in the suburbs together with the indistinct hieroglyphs of family history: the never-knowable, the only surmisable, biographical interpretations. From its depths she can hear her own echo, the sound of bones being rattled around, the off-key tone of clunky incomplete stories. Words on paper may be insubstantial material to use for work about building. The solidity of the house stands against the perceived unreliability of family stories, its construction assumed to be sound. The precarious structure of the family, the tentative, equivocal narratives contrast sharply with the physicality of the house. The framework of the house forms a skeleton for anything she can tell about the life lived in the house at Ennerdale Drive, for what she's seen and heard and what she hasn't. It's entirely circumstantial, pieced together with her limited supply of intimate knowledge, largely tangential. The sting of absence and separation might be turned into an advantage of distance. Anything not directly witnessed, anything that cannot be corroborated can be described in the Turkish language, as Orhan Pamuk recounts in *Istanbul*, using a tense that exists for the personally unseen and the imaginary, for dreams and myths and hearsay. Though this tense is untranslatable, it is not lost in translation: it amounts to the phrase 'or so I've been told'.

Examining the narrative excavations of the past through the prism of a material object, from roof tiles to floor joists, characters make their entrance in snippets of tale balanced in its interstices holding it all together like mortar. Endless traces are deposited to be picked up, sniffed out, stuck together somehow to construct a whole studded with scar tissue, crooked seams drawn on. Someone is brutally, desperately salvaging a narrative from a fragment, turning a fragment into a narrative whole. Not letting it alone. And who might that be? On demolition sites houses are taken down and interior walls revealed with the perspective flattened, hollowed out. Brick and joist toothy outlines, remains of wall and floor levels, ragged flutters of wallpapers are exposed to the light and the rude public gaze with a brutal flash. The bald spot where the sink used to be, the outline of dirt that defines a mirror shape, a course of tiles with nothing left to edge, flimsy wooden housings where white goods used to stand, wires and cables disabled, hanging. That rough carpentry was always meant to be concealed. The markers of life lived and gone, those lives lost, their space ruptured: the stories are soon to be dismantled and shifted pell-mell into a skip. The skin itself, seeming so windproof and washable, is revealed as the most tender of veneers, endangered, and in need of the shelter its removal has stripped off.

Every exposed detail, the corners, the dirt, the color schemes are stripped naked without the protective coating between interior and exterior and a grubby tenderness is revealed. Secrets are aired and oxidized. An explosion of disclosure leaks out into the common realm as the room is first opened out. No sweet, poignant rest happens here after the struggle of leaving life behind. No nostalgic, drunken passing around of charming versions of who and when and how. It's brutal, and the evisceration is not only physical. This is a room, a house, a wall striped of meaning. It's an obscenity, something not supposed to be visible. If its physical presence was audible, it would be the sound of the building shrieking and wincing, as it flails around trying to cover itself. It's roughly turned inside out, innards showing, dripping. All that dirt, all that intimate fluid mingling, indiscriminate and dangerous. It's an abjection late of brick and timber. It's what no one wants to see, the rudely exposed, scraped open inner layers, and what everyone is hungry to gawp at and equally desperate to turn away from, to shield the eyes.

Unfaded shapes of original, unexposed paintwork show up how overdue is redecoration. The patterns for living, however haphazard, existing in every home are interrupted, fatally, and permanently. There's nothing for the respiratory and circulatory systems to breathe in or pump around, only evacuation and hemorrhaging out. Hollows and cavities, punctured surfaces, seeping residues of occupation, are what remain. The weathered inscriptions of habitation leave timely impressions of wear and tear. Private notes of failure clang behind closed doors. Nothing is proof against the cool breeze of public access. Now the doors are redundant, now there's no wall left with a space to be filled, no frame for it to sit in. The hinges are left loose for now, no longer choked with paint. All the stories of what happened here pass into another, harsher realm of publicity, licking its lips, knuckles bright with the wind and cold. All nuance and meander has blown away. The vacuum left by the unsung and the uninhabited causes the house to implode. All fall down. The stories are no longer contained on their own stage but without a holding location or a storyteller to hand them over or pass them on they have no currency, no lasting shape or value.

Free to make the house, the relationships, into whatever she want, that's what she's been told. But it's no blank slate. It's almost too crowded for new versions to find space for an airing on the page. Wiping it clean and starting over was never an option, writing over the top is the only way to make fast an impression. Flooding it with new words, scratching new letters over the old graffiti. It might all have been true once. All the stories of the house are relived and rewritten visibly, without regard for earlier renditions. Looking at the walls tells that, tells all that. Read it. Nothing is saved. An equal integrity attaches to every version and none is ever finished without tomorrow's story scrawled on top and yesterday's still visible beneath, over the fading traces of the day before and last week and all the way back. This was a set once, a domestic stage of lived space, peopled by the stories that are now hanging ragged, with only traces left of epics, mysteries and comedies. All the stories that have been trodden into these boards are now open to the curious, uncaring gaze of the elements and passers-by bypassing unwanted emotion, curdled and undissipated, highly visible but nothing to attach to. When they finally pull down the little palaces the stories will still be there, still unfinished, deadends full of holes. That's the happy ending. Stop now.

Exhibit 7: Plastic picture

There's nothing to show. There is no plastic picture. I don't have it any more. If I had it, the picture would act as a stand-in (an understudy?) for the memory of a visit, together with reports from people old enough to remember the visit or to have taken me there. A present without presence; a memory standing in for an object standing in for a memory. It was a one-piece molded plastic thing with a beige-colored 'frame' and integral stand. Photographic emulsion on plastic (or on to anything other than photographic paper) seems quite technologically advanced for the time. The legend 'A Present from Bristol Zoo' was stamped in gold italic script, I'm guessing, along the bottom of the printed frame. A photograph of a ring-tailed lemur was printed on to the front. My present from Bristol Zoo was bought for me on a visit there during my dad's tenure as head of the Bristol Old Vic Theatre School. I don't remember any of this: him being there, him being away from home, or visiting him in Bristol. I don't remember, either, the much more exciting and significant event of going on a day out to Bristol zoo.

Some would have it that a memento is in fact a mark of forgetting. I'm not letting this one get away: cheap souvenir plastic picture as a mark of forgetting. So the absence of a memento involves an act of remembrance. Even in its absence, especially then, the picture retains what Walter Benjamin describes as the auratic promise that it speaks of the past, a promise that it cannot fulfill. An auratic object can never satisfy the desire to recover the memory and it pulls you back over and over. There's no external object here, no repetition either, only a compulsive reminder of footsteps left in the sand.

According to Deleuze, the absence of the object makes it into the construct of the fossil. I'm still drawn back again. I'm led firmly by (my own) hand into a territory I fear and long for, dragging my feet for extra postponement. Again the absence is as meaningful as the thing itself but the plastic picture is different from other unfound items like the caricature. It belonged to me and stayed with me as long as any other childhood toy, maybe longer as it represented a simple link to my dad. It's a fossil of a memory that I can no longer retrieve, my own reminder that I was there in Bristol. I was where my dad was. It was evidence I can point to, proof without giving anything away. I was there and so was he. Still I need to truffle out the markers, or the memories of them.

The picture will have degraded and cracked and the color faded but plastic doesn't decompose. It hangs around for decades, refusing to disappear, a souvenir repeating from another time and place. With this knot of histories leading to the arousal of an intensity of other memories, a plastic picture makes a perfect fossil. It can lie in landfill for a lifetime, blankly. Way out of proportion to its intrinsic value, its magnetic pull resides in the very inability to satisfy the desire to recover the memory. It will never go away and leave you. Or me. Its existence, or my knowledge of its existence, brings forth no memories, instead suggestions of other places to look, for other objects and other strands of narrative. In a narrative of loss and memory, incomplete pictures are twice missing. Guilana Bruno suggests that the picture is an object turned into a narrative by way of emotion, creating a memory to stand in for what I don't have, an emotionally articulated object. To start to remember, to embark on an excavation of reminiscence, is sweet and bitter. Since there's no plastic picture to be found, I have to look further. What's turned over is about my dad's time at Bristol.

It's this memory of a fossil which leads me to further investigation, to an archive and to a published commemorative history of the Bristol Old Vic School. I read that my dad was there for four terms from 1961 to 1963 so I was maybe two years old when he took up the job. The commentary in the book dwells heavily on the gravity of his injuries, it seems to me, and their impact on his work at the school. Disability awareness in the 1960s amounted to being kind and respectful, treating the handicapped and the crippled with sympathy. That was as good as it got. It was the norm to define the person by their disability and not much more, even though everyday experience of the effects of disability on family life was commonplace after the First and Second World Wars. War-injured men were pitied, while gratitude for their sacrifice was assumed and expressed as standard. (Inter)National efforts turn into individual sacrifices, burdens that must be borne personally – as my dad did along with the rest – and quietly, and in my memory at least, he wasn't quiet at all.

I experience a lack of daughterly gratitude when faced with a depiction that emphasizes that 'despite' his injuries he was likeable and charismatic and that 'his great voice was intact' even if the rest of him wasn't. It takes me some time to pass through this, sitting quietly enraged at this stranger speaking ill of my dead, in the British Library Reading Room taking notes.

Reports in the book from the students at Bristol are mixed: included are comments that he brought unusual and stimulating ideas into the place; that he was considered a bit of a ham, too old-school;

that he focused on staging productions and let everything else rot; that he insisted they work without costumes on the basis that character and authority come from within. He established a Directors' course and installed radio facilities. This seems like quite a lot in less than two years. I can see how much criticism comes with the job, it must be thankless being a director of any institution. At my school it was the size of his presence and the frisson of his reception as the sole man at daytime functions that was the cause of my embarrassment and pride, not his disabilities. I probably thought he could do anything even though I could see that he couldn't. My friends weren't old enough to be cruel; it's not that you don't notice. He was special (and that included specially embarrassing) because he was my dad and that was what mattered.

There's too much in this book for me to know, and none of it's right, even when it is. There's (yet) another story about how he was injured. Accident with faulty firearm? 'Friendly fire'? Vehicle driving over mine? It's easy to see how during wartime the precise circumstance of a soldier's injury might get mangled. When the locations reported are Italy, Germany or the US, that's too many stories and a stretch too far. A cleaned-up version of how he died is part of their narrative: when he was learning his lines late one night. That's supposed to be a respectful, touching comfort, the way any actor would want to go. And a lie too. You can guess the rest. There's no more story to tell after this.

These recollections cover some of the years of my real actual honest-as-I-can-manage memories of him. There are too many ways in which I don't want to know all this or this pain that's self-inflicted. That's what this amounts to: the selfishness of the seven-year-old who doesn't want him to be anything else except her dad; and the selfishness of the 47-year-old driven to keep looking for something just in case, sentencing herself to be unnerved by reports good or bad. I don't want to know it from a book that I don't think is very good, not from this stranger of an author, and not from an author I know either that he was 'exhausted by the pain he lived with'.

Every time you dust off a memory, the story's different as it's viewed in a new present. My picture of him, the construct of my little-girl memories, has already been broken and put back together. The picture proves to me that I was there and that he was; yes that's me, part of his life beyond the world of production stills and publicity leaflets. I'm not short on memories of spending time with my dad, but this object is material proof. Or it would be. And sometimes nothing else will do. Objects stand in for what's missing: a house, a plastic picture. What's been lost: the image, the voice, the family story. The list of what's missing isn't long, it's about the amount of space left uninhabited. But there is comfort yet, in this no-comfort. There's comfort in the discovery that the word comes from the Latin to strengthen, as well as meaning to console and soothe. There's comfort in telling, in passing on; and the other comforts of storytelling; the pleasures of suspension of disbelief, of listening, of expectation, of form. Finishing, shutting off, there would be comfort in all that too: the bounded tale, the resolution. Or so she's been told.

Henry as Hamlet and the plastic picture are unavailable as evidence then, both have eluded the power of the detective. She never knows what she's going to be able to find except it will always be the unexpected. Sometimes what can be found is part of what Stephen Barber calls a diaspora of memory and loss, finding and losing at the same time. Occasionally the lazy distraction of re-searching a source that's already come up negative gives up more direct results: newly found materials, rather than those refound through her trademark archival misfiling practices. Archives are not static either. What did not appear, now does; what was not there before, is. Henry's name comes up in a website search memory when she goes back again to the National Sound Archive website at the British Library. This time around the National Sound Archive holds 18 recordings by Henry, although some of these are duplicates that have been catalogued twice. This discovery happens when she's writing about what can't be found, the recognition of the values of not knowing and unexpected sources of consolation. Freshly catalogued recordings constitute some kind of substitute for the *Hamlet* cutting.

On this occasion the lacunae of the archive take an opposite form: not so much gap as duplication, and taking a place that could be filled by another item. Twice-over speeches from *Hamlet*, a Tennyson poem and a 1914 morale booster for the First World War troops are part of the 18 but even so, it's a good haul. A handful, *Hamlet* speeches among them, are marked as available to listen now in mp3. All highly accessible except the technology isn't up to it and the site is too busy, so the electronic access keeps timing out or the server is not responding. 'Available now' is dependent on location, the time is dependent on space. It's an internal service: the site catalogue is available remotely but Soundserver, the digitized sound service the archive uses, allows onsite access only. She makes the appointment, orders the recordings in advance. She's assigned a carrel in the Rare Music and Books Department. It's cool and very calm inside compared to the crazed humidity of Euston Road on a July evening, even compared to the more populous reading rooms in the library. The only other time she's been to this department was to look at her grandfather's love letters and family entries in *Spotlight*. She's not expecting a repeat performance of her reaction to that material. It was a someone-else's-diary, parents-having-sex kind of thing and a research-cool wave of confirmation at the same time.

Of the 18 recordings, she has the Tennyson poem already on audiotape; five are duplicates, one is identified only as 'His Master's Voice 1457/Product'; and one is lost. The missing recording, a shellac 78rpm, is a rendition of the speech that begins 'Look here upon this picture' (*Hamlet* III iv). This could hardly be better. This is almost more exciting than finding the caricature. But still, there is no picture, either as a thumbnail in the recording catalogue or elsewhere, at least not the one she was looking for. The fact that the National Sound Archive holds recordings of Henry reading speeches from *Hamlet* and that they are lost, serves to change her supposition about the caricature being him in that role into a certainty, despite the lack of documentation to guarantee either that the recordings were production-related or that the production was *Hamlet*. She knows she's not the only person who gets as excited about what's missing from the archive as what it holds, she can't be.

But she doesn't get any kind of thrill, no reaction at all really, to hearing his voice and she wasn't expecting that. Again and again, seven times in all, she feels very little response to the man himself. It's no longer about grandfather as vocal embodiment: her interest lay in how his voice was reproduced, in the production, in the context. Even if she wasn't getting to the end of her fascination with him, access is already compromised because these are renderings from other formats. That's what she's thinking, trying to keep in mind her family and detective obligations. Hearing the archivist say 'National Sound Archive dubbing of BBC archive disks on loan' whets her appetite more than the man himself. Her interest is caught when she hears that some of the recordings are taken from single- and double-sided shellac 78s; some from reel-to-reel audiotape; one from a radio program; and one is an unpublished HMV test pressing, probably acetate or shellac. These materials and technologies are now obsolete but Henry was used as an exemplar for new technology testing. Advances in sound and image recording technologies really did have enormous influence on his career. She's finding him in pieces, and the pieces are sometimes connected. Soon there will be more than enough pieces of him to stop looking.

On the first shellac recording played for her, she listens primarily to the crackle, so pronounced it sounds like rice being poured. It's Edgar Allan Poe's 'The Bells'. Henry alters his voice depending on the kind of bell: tinkling bells, long-vowel deep bells and loud alar(u)m bells. With the euphony and the rhyme, it sounds like all the awfulness of Christmas. It's quite testing to listen to it. She wonders at how restrained he sounds speaking the speeches from Shakespeare plays; at how many epigrams embedded into the English language come from phrases in his plays; at how strange it is right there then to hear a play read rather than viewing it, sound no visual; and at the generational shift when she hears Henry's tone and accent in the two *Hamlet* speeches, how old he sounds. A startling Englishness inherent in a performance of poetry set to Elgar sounds to her like a misrepresentation of his more internationally diverse family-to-come. It was the first performance of this Elgar piece, broadcast on Radio 3 in 1915 in two 16-minute recordings of him contributing to a two-part program presented by Malcolm Ruthven on Elgar and the gramophone. It's like poetry with sound effects from school music lessons: 'the sound of the drum, the sound of the bugle'. Mrs Elgar noted in her diary: 'Mr Ainley to lunch. Very nice.' An HMV recording, 'Why Britain is at war' is largely taken from a letter from *The Times* to squash popular opinion that the war is an avoidable and expensive affair that would be better left in the lap of the quarrelling foreigners who caused it. He appeals to the better nature of the population through invocations to the good name of the country, and the importance of safeguarding nation, empire and the freedom of democracies in Europe.

Henry is relatively low-key and plain spoken in most of these recordings by comparison with the Tennyson poem that she found so startling. He was an actor, after all, no penny-in-slot ham orator. She chose not to credit this, on the basis of this one recording (a performance) and one caricature (unfound). She couldn't let him be. Now that he's become visually and aurally familiar to her, maybe she can let him be great and let him alone.

In the generations across the globe affected by the conflicts, the First and Second World Wars put paid to the possibility of a simple and cozy family life. In the everyday drama of the domestic the parts are acted out in works that the players are not familiar with, in a plot they know only sketchily, whose first and last scenes are beyond their imagination. Characters are born into roles influenced by forces over which they have no sway, impacted by stories they may never understand, may never even hear. In this version of family, serial bouts of marriage and extra-marital liaisons, both with resultant children, continent-hopping, success, untimely death and migration, are further disruptions to that possibility. The disapproval and taboos attaching to adultery, divorce and illegitimacy may be outmoded but their effects endure. The reach of their stain penetrates deep and wide and is sustained through the status of mythology. Anna Massey says in her biography *Telling Some Tales* that, coming from an acting family, 'divorce, drama and infidelity were woven into the fabric of our lives.' Following in family footsteps can be skewed and blinkered for that's all there is, it's all anyone knows. Putting on identities, playing out scenes, learning lines: all the language is there already. Anna Massey suggests that revelation has a particular quality when there are actors in the family. It's ordinary everyday stuff.

Like the mythological tale, the family is ordered round a central figure or location. When that core is missing or removed another tale of added force and questionable accuracy has to fill the vacuum and stand as substitute. The stories from within and outside the house are instruments of reactivation, aftershock reverberating long after the event. The backwash of the waywardness and habits of others can only continue to be visited on the lives of the new generation.

A rupture was created within the fabric of the immediate family, and within everything else. It's a rupture that has to stand in as an explanation for uncles not seen for 20 years, marriages and divorces unheard of, for absent brothers and fathers. No lumpy darning or visits to remembered houses, or phone calls or excavations can mend it: the cycles of family life are distorted into ashes and fallout. There's no coming back from it. Sketching inwards from the margins to fill out the skeleton and shape the inner spaces, the subjects emerge from the empty framework. As a family, they lack a center, there's no singular venue to perform in together. It's an absence that has to be written around as the cue. Only Henry lingers and he's not even there.

Sensory impression and memory count for more than measurement and certainty here. The precisions of building construction are less important, and since they are unavailable, that's fortuitous. The original plans of the house would tell less about Ant's life than the paths worn in the carpet and the arrangement of furniture in the rooms. 2 Ennerdale Drive became a place to live as it became their place to live, created through a convergence of planning and development and speculation and dreams and ambition and progress and interference. Data can be read off the house endlessly, but it keeps its secrets. Circling round all the stories of the town planner, the developer, the house, the family, the actor, the writer eventually creates some kind of edifice. It's vulnerable because delicate and multilayered, because its limits, if there are beginnings and ends to be found, are uncertain and shifting. The story doesn't all come together at the end this time, with dangling threads caught up and dropped stitches chased in.

Using remembered sites and dream sites, the house and its stories are a reconstruction of a version of the past in the present, excavated into existence. The physicality of the house as a built object on the street doesn't make it any more substantial than an architecture of stories. It's no more sturdy than a three-dimensional story, a paper-model tale, a performance of an architecture of writing. The material tears and crumples and rots and disintegrates. Words fade and the constructions they make are carried from reader to reader. Their marks can't last; their meaning, ever changed, persists. There's precious little truth in it but the subject endures for all that and it's not the stories that get pulled down. The edifice of writing about 2 Ennerdale Drive ensures the house's lasting existence as it becomes another work, beginning with marks on paper and an idea with an endless life. It won't perish through lack of use, unlike family connections.

The suburbs contain and display; the house acts as holder for the raw material of stories. 2 Ennerdale Drive is a backdrop, a hanging paper flat. It's a trigger for remembrance and invention of situations and events. The house is at once a material fabrication and one on which to hang other constructions. It's a house that will eventually subside into London clay, moisture in the northern European climate playing damp havoc with Laing's honorably spec'd materials but still sturdy enough for the origination and containment of unfinished stories. No.2 exists strongly enough in a leaky, obsolescent way to shelter the imaginary. It's a repository for recollection and its re-engraving; the memories that can be attached to it are fixed in space, flimsy markers of stability. The enduring qualities of the paper fiction and an architecture of writing accrue value next to the fragility of buildings. The house supports an insubstantiality, an inauthenticity; anonymity causes it to do a disappearing act, its faded promise is worn away, tarnished. And yet the stories aren't themselves delicate, even though their subjects and their relationships may be broken or dislocated.

$$\bullet \bullet \bullet$$

You?! You're not a detective! Where's the crime? What's the evidence? Where's the harm, tell me that? What's the story? Who do you think you are? You're not a detective. She keeps telling herself, that's for sure. No secret there. She goes on: You're a liar, you, raising expectations, giving out false hopes. That's the harm. You're supposed to lighten the mystery, not manufacture it. You're not solving anything, not even trying to get the facts right. You're making chaos, not making sense. You can't leave off trying to make something of it, can you? You have to let it be, let it alone.

You're setting up yourself and everybody else, it's no way for a detective to behave. Mistaking candles for fireworks, draughts for hurricanes: the clues come after the disclosures with you. It's not how to do this, anyone can see that and you ought to be able to tell yourself. She can't stop, can't let herself alone. You ought to be filling in the missing pieces, rounding off the edges, following through, winding it up.

The detective lays out hypotheses like laying out pages to see what connections can be made, finds all the pieces, or enough of them, to fit together to get to an ending, for an eventual judgment. But you? You're sowing unease and conjecture, celebrating the opposite. You're not trying to establish meaning and sense or follow leads. You construct pieces just so that they won't fit, you favor misalignment and all of it to build deeper into the cracks. And for what? Where does it get you? You're not a detective. It's just me. I must be the guilty one then if I'm not the detective.

She's right, I'm not a detective. 'She's' right? I'm right. I was never looking for answers, not really, Leave me and my detective self in my smear of dreams and fictions. I belong to it and it to me and she and me and I. I can find or form the selvedge and unravel it again, as I want it to be. I can keep telling tales without giving anything away because the story changes every time it's delivered on to the next listener. The story is remade with every telling, just as the architecture of the house is changed through each use. Someone said I was cheating at patience. I'm catching voices in the building, using a detective story to piece together how, as Beatrice Colomina has it, 'space is constructed as interior'. Telling the tales passes on everything on, slightly scrambled through the lines of whispering and so refashioned to an extent almost unrecognizable. The original stays put while each version is verbally overridden in the next telling. If doubts are left still about the endurance of the successive versions, the delicate fabric of stories, paper or digital, there's nothing more to be done now. It never goes away. Telling lies, keeping secrets; all the stories are lies and so are all the secrets.

If all the world's a stage, then every home has one. What a theater involves compresses easily into sound, image, text, building: a stage, seating, playwright, curtains, actors, an audience, a script, props, lines, sound effects, sets. For a brief moment when, no longer fascinated or repelled, there's no doubt about who the director is but then I'm back sitting avid and fearful about what comes next. So I'm going to click fingers and heels. Do it now. Let it happen. I'm a storyteller, not a detective. I'm retreading facts and memories for my own purposes, making fictions about the real, with documented evidence, personal and cultural memory, association and response to architectural fact. Call it rethreading or repatterning the integrity of the material. When I know what I'm looking for, I won't need to look. For now, I'm after something or somebody. I'm sifting through circumstantial evidence. I'm making something of it, yes. I'm showing how far it can go, how long I can stretch it out. I can't stop visiting the dead-ends yet and the open spaces, running my fingers through it, looking to find an end in a search for the indefinable and unknowable.

Chapter 5

Lost and found revisited

The residents of 2 Ennerdale Drive might have had sufficient choice and few enough options to make a home in Colindale but for Pam and Harry it won't do. She'll have to find somewhere else for them to live. Where were they supposed to go? Henry could be placed in residence where Angela Carter houses her character Melchior Hazard and stages his receptions. Everything she imagines about Henry could be staged in just such places; he needs a baronial pile, an extravagant, overblown fiction of inter-locking platforms for his all-day, every-day permanent perfor-mance. She had imagined her family into being and they needed houses to live in, an elaborate set on which to play out the stories of their lives. Henry doesn't need anyone to find him somewhere to live or to create any grandiose country villa as a backdrop for his Lord of the Manor role: these are places that already exist.

Henry lived for some time at Chart Lodge in Kent, on the outskirts of the village of Little Chart. She went looking for the house for the first time on a balmy early autumn day, driving through the Kent landscape full of rolling hills and horsey paddocks separating large houses with walled land around them. She's on her way to a party after this expedition which was carefully scheduled so that any disappointment can be swerved around with the knowledge that the cross-county trip had another purpose entirely. The village of Little Chart is set on a hill with a green at its center and a pub at the bottom, full of Sunday dinner eaters and a clutch of men drinking in their local. The landlord points her in the direction of a man at the bar who's known as the local history expert. He tells her that the house is up at the other end of the village, at the top of the hill. She's an outsider, even before she start driving on to private property and snooping about in their lovely light that doesn't quite fall across the county. She's still the unwelcome spy. She drives into a couple of places substantial enough to be what she's looking for. She finds a South Lodge but no Chart: and this is Little, not Great, Chart so it doesn't take long to exhaust the possibilities.

More queries, more research: the name of the house has been changed to Chart Court. Another trip for the new year, another foray. The house is on the road to Pluckley, so far outside Little Chart that it wouldn't count as the same place for a townie like her. On the approach she spies in the distance what looks like the turrets of a castle in front of a pair of oasts decked out in colorful heraldic topknots, cocked like pistols. She amuses herself by thinking that the castle she can see is Henry's but it's the oasts that are her destination, next to a church ruin.

Chart Lodge or Chart Court or whatever they call it now (she's behaving proprietorially, as if it's her house whose name has been tinkered with) is a house that has taken the name of its location, as though the head man lives there. It's all a put-on, of course. It's just a house with pretensions, a house whose owners want to play at living in the village manor. Its site outside the village constitutes a cold-shouldering of the everyday life around the hub of shop or pub or post office and embraces instead the status conferred by proximity to the church. More than the name of the house has changed. The information boards for St Mary's Church reveal that the medieval church on the site, one of only two interdenominational churches in England, was destroyed by a 'doodlebug' (V1 bomb) on 16 August 1944 and that the house also had to be substantially rebuilt after the bomb damage. Now the house is hemmed in by other vernacular housing as the immediate area has been developed into a small tourist complex. As she drives past she sees Chart Court Stables, Chart Court Barn and The Granary next door, which looks like it has been converted into comfortably expensive country holiday accommodation, as well as Chart Court, which could itself be several houses under one roof.

Here it is. She doubles back to pull up on the gravel drive and admire the impeccable hedge and think about how to get at what's beyond it. As she rings the bell on the numbercode entry system she listens for a factotum shuffling out to be rude to unannounced callers. She can almost hear the sound of Henry amusing himself by researching a role between parts. She may have started getting used to the sound of his voice but she's forever distanced from his position in society. No one is on duty answering the door today though, staff or otherwise. Through a gap in the fence she can see a corner of a herringbone-laid brick outbuilding beyond a trim lawn. She only wants a glimpse, she says. This is a venue for her, never mind Harry and Whatshername. But she would always want just a bit more. She wants in. She wants to see it all for herself.

From the churchyard end of the house she gets a little more of a view, over a thick fence of brambles and nettles and ivy before a further guard of evergreen hedge. She can see shuttered windows, CCTV cameras, one car and garage space for several more. This is perfect. This is where he lived; this is where he lived for some time with her grandmother, two public constructs of their day, and members of her family by paper more than blood. She can see their house and she can't get in so it's hers to ramraid on the page. It is perfect. She contents herself for now with digging up a few factoids to build upon from online estate agent sites. At the turn of the 19th century the house belonged to a prominent racehorse owner, another profession based on the mastery of spectacle. It is his racing colors that determine the red and green of the oast cowls. Every other oast house in the country must have white cowls, Chart Court remains exempt from this regulation and has to sport the red and the green permanently. The last time Chart Court had exchanged hands, it went to the first viewer for £875,000; planning permission for floodlights, general updating and extension of the existing stables was granted in 2006. Unless the racing magnate's bets and horseflesh went bad and he had to move house in a hurry, he was probably the owner of Chart Court immediately before Henry. His professional interests can be taken to account for the extensive stabling provision and the tang of horses, because naturally they kept their own for family and guests to ride about the country and over the Downs.

Inside, from the period of Henry's occupation almost a century earlier, she's seeing a welter of beams, thatch and terrazzo, velvet and marble: another ridiculous and now all-too real confection. Vaulted ceilings, inglenooks, leather-padded library walls, dressing rooms, chandeliers, silk drapes, anterooms, galleried atriums and mezzanines, ballrooms and bedrooms of a dimension, fit for the most lofty lord of the manor and his retainers, dogs and ladies. Then there's the suite of studies for the writing of novels (and living them) and the learning of lines (ditto). And endless small rooms dedicated to endless, unseen purposes: dank kitchens with high windows, minuscule sculleries by back staircases. Outdoors are tennis courts, croquet lawn, summerhouses, rose gardens, sun terraces, pools and ponds, pavilions and marquees, secret gardens, covered walkways, swards of green, a long gravel drive for crunching along in a splendid new motor car or churning up under horses' hooves. A fleet of servants, properly costumed and working good accents are on call for a (pre)enactment of a prototype *Upstairs Downstairs*. She's off and away. But this house is not that big. This is one for Melchior Hazard, not Henry Ainley.

One of the redundant hop houses at Chart Court could be converted into a small domestic playhouse. It's an obvious choice, if ahead of its time. And so their house becomes another venue for public performance by provision as well as private domesticity. Now the oast is a receptacle for stories that may run and run rather than a building to dry anything, but still a platform to wring out all they have, to air a dramatic moment. He was good at that. They might be too busy watching themselves to look out at anyone else. Their house is the theater of the world, not a mere box in it. It's a house for being famous off-duty. The life of the family is a constant round of striking poses, static tableaux of classic scenes. Domestic theatricals by professionals with non-professional family members dragged into service. Everyone can take part and derive enjoyment and education, whether as audience, as players or as critics. Photographic mementos of these happy afternoons at home could be supplied by prominent amateurs, with the advertising value payment enough.

Henry might try a part on for size, away from the glare of the West End audience and the press johnnies. It's the perfect spot to invite other off-duty actors to lead in exclusive productions in a unique theater-in-the-roundel-space, with its conical roof and inhouse colors. From his position as an elder in the profession, a generous casting of younger actors in leading roles at the Chart Theatre bolsters his position. He glitters even more brightly in rural abeyance. Lord of the Manor could experiment to his heart's content. He can indulge, he can take risks. He plays at making a hobby of his profession. Of course it's more than a profession, it's the life and the living, and his life. He can almost hear the rehearsals already, imagine the place transformed into a cozy 100-seat auditorium, with lights and plush seats and even printed programs. *A Midsummer Night's Dream* in the oast would be the thing, of course! The children enjoy being pressed into making programmes and tickets, little keepsakes for those who attend. He likes them to use the red and the green of the oast colors. Perhaps some of the stage writers might like to provide a piece specially written for the place. Some of the London press would likely be pleased enough to come down here and be entertained for the evening.

The dimensions of the oast bring new staging challenges: the teacup of stage, the single entrance and exit, the absence of any backstage space or facilities, the maw of ceiling space that swallows the spoken word. Though cozy in size, the ex-oast's prized properties of draught and ventilation are never quite overcome. Neither is the smell to be forgotten, quite lingering, and something of a distraction. For the summer performance, he can throw open the specially widened doors of the oasthouse and mark out a stage on the lawn with an auditorium to seat more than a handful of spectators. The oast can serve as both backstage and part of the set, with some decoration and imagination. Maybe later on, he thinks, one of these damp-stinking but fine outbuildings can be fitted out as another kind of showplace. An exhibition might be presented, a permanent display of theatrical memorabilia, photographs, drawings, programs, annotated playscripts, props and costumes and the like. Then it might be taken on later for the county perhaps, even for the nation. Something of an archive.

The thing is, though, this isn't the house where Henry lived. Chart Court could have worked very well, it's true, but (with a sudden concern for verisimilitude) it's not the one. It was a bad call, misleading information. It's the wrong house in the wrong village. It's still in Kent, at Seal Chart, not Little Chart, and the village is further west, closer to Sevenoaks rather than edging on to Ashford. Seal Chart is the source of the phone number in Henry Ainley's *Spotlight* entry of 1926: KEMsing, putting a house to the number. Kemsing is a larger village a few miles away, over the other side of the A25, which is strung with drive-by villages lining the way as outsize road transport strains though. The previous recce for Chart Court/Lodge was in spring time when the canopy of leaf coverage overhead was a welcome shelter from sharp light, now it's autumn again for visit number three and she feels an instant coolness once the sunlight is blocked out. The way is lined with big houses too, any of these would do for the staging of the family photo opp: gentleman farmer Ainley at the stable gate with family, children on horses, feeding chickens. That sort of thing. She's not guessing this time, she's seen one of those pictures.

The house at Seal Chart was easy to find in the end, overlooking the two wrongly identified suspects. Even then, she took the wrong exit from the motorway, too anxious, too early. But when she pulled over to check the map she realized she'd turned off on to the A25 that runs through Seal. She had come the scenic route. It's all so simple on the map. Signs for 'Heart of Kent' are everywhere, which in planting terms stands for a greenery of mature trees, a very English late summer color, lots of oak.

'The two-floor nineteenth-century house is set in woodland in Seal Chart village in an Area of Outstanding Natural Beauty, converted into apartments in the 1970s. It's big on window details, dormers and bays with leaded panes, an east–west aspect for varied light throughout the day. Includes brick outbuildings (now mostly garages).' The detailed prose of the estate agent's details presents the house, any house, as an empty set, awaiting occupation. She can see, a while away yet, more oasts (well it is Kent) and turrets, roughly where she reckons Seal Chart to be. But that's not it, not this time. The 'turrets' are the fifteenth-century ragstone tower of St Peter and St Paul Church in Seal, the village next to Seal Chart. There are oasts right next door to the house, others entirely from those spied from the car. Chart Court is hidden from the road but signage tells her twice over that this is the right place, if she hadn't already chosen to believe this is the one. Three visits, enough. And there's that phone number as well as the admission of the false trail by her source.

It's done, over, and beware of the dog. A gravel drive is lined with 'ancient oak' and rhododendrons. She's found the house. It's finished and she doesn't want to see any more of it. She doesn't need to. Must have been someone else who kept on looking. She's here though, so she circles round the loop of drive and wishes she'd stuck with the estate agent's details, succinct and suggestive. Now that she has seen the house, now that she knows it exists, she can imagine the lines of cars in the drive full of visitors and audience, the blissful and stormy home life, the late-night drives home after the show. Now the detective has found the places where the fantasy family lived, no need to make any more of them up or even see them.

Set in its silence of woodlands, a space of tamed wildness, Seal Chart must have been guarded as a place of separation and safety for the two of them, for as long as it lasted. Safe both from the tongues of propriety and those of profession, the delivery of lines on a stage could resume. There's the whiff of the secret about it, something ungoverned or ungovernable, firmly within society yet beyond metropolitan disapproval. An imaginary place after all, set low in the countryside, almost subsumed within it, a bubble in a sea of green. There's an innocence and a pungent sexual overtone with all that teeming fecundity. It's a country residence that allows them to pose as themselves, offstage.

Seal Chart operated as an arcadian space for Henry and Bijou, a place of safety away from the harshness of the city; the idea and maybe even the daily reality of Ennerdale Drive might have served the same function for aunties and for suburban dwellers or potential residents of the suburbs in general. Arcadias, like suburbias, can be maintained only within a catalogue of exclusions and rules, whatever the parameters, whoever polices them and this one is firmly tweaked. As Pam learned, Arcadia is more than cross-dressing nymphs in lush forests. It's a defined area where different rules apply, a temporal tear in a parallel universe or a breathing space.

The houses exist, that's true enough, but the previous life they contained can only survive in scraps, their social relations as histories. They exist in the imaginary always. The building, a tallish story concretized, acts as testimony for the life within and without. The physicality of the house might insist on its endurance as an image, if not as a construction in its original state. Tales and memory of family operate differently: bursts of stills, snapshots in no particular order bring on a sickly sinking feeling. Rose-colored glasses aren't to hand. Next frame please.

●●●

I'm standing in the entrance to a hall where a party is in the final stages of being organized for later that day. This is a grand house, it is the kind of place that Pam and her creator might have been used to either visiting or being excluded from. The house belongs to someone else, but it's comfortable enough for me to be here. I'm allowed. It never becomes clear whose house it is but it's hard to imagine anyone living a day-to-day mundane existence here. This house is like a stage set because it really is one, with furniture and fittings from a period drama that was shot here. It's a location that has been lent to us. One of the assembled, or the later-to-be assembled, is filming here. We're keeping it in the family. Whoever it belongs to, my mum is having her party here in the ballroom. The place is a whirl of pillars, marble steps, columns and statues, acanthus moldings and carved cornicing, a great pastiche of a stately home to play on forever.

Through an enormous arch I can see my mum presiding over proceedings. I have never watched her do this before. Large round tables are being covered and dressed by legions of staff, both in starched white linen, where people will be sitting (to watch something on a stage or a performance or an award ceremony?). Setting and atmosphere are building in front of my eyes. Later on staff will offer food and drink, park cars and take coats. A gallery looks out over a formal garden surrounded by tamed woodlands. Inside, huge portraits of god-knows-who, dignitaries and ancestors, line the paneled staircase curving broadly into the cavernous mosaic-floored hall. There are candle chandeliers, their tiny flames already lit. And those who take the trouble to notice will see that the chandelier in the ballroom has been updated with electric candle bulbs to avoid accidents with wax even though it has so far to fall it would be set cold should it ever hit anyone.

Tonight people will throng in the soft light as they line up to deliver greetings to the hostess, and the host, if there is one. Because it's not my dad, he isn't here. 'We' are all here. The 'we' I want to see, that is. My dad and my eldest brother are absent. I'm not giving them access to this dream of a party for reasons of my own. Tom Baker, unrelated but sometime one of us, is somehow allowed to be here. In an oneirically fuelled impossibility, he's sitting next to Henry Ainley who died long before Tom had met my dad, before my dad met my mum and before my brother, whom I have so generously allowed to be present at someone else's party, was born. This is all too much. Nausea is threatening to knock me off my feet, or maybe it's too much excitement, a haze of anticipation. And I think, oh that's a bad pairing. That seating arrangement won't work, those two won't get on. Henry is bored already, sitting next to someone he's never met and what were they thinking of, placing him next to this person?

Since it's a house to be famous in, it comes with a cast of guests for putting on a show and a gossip columnist in attendance and a staircase for making an entrance. The guests are not going to arrive in fancy dress or at least they don't call it that but you won't be able to tell who anyone is. Henry is amusing himself by casting everyone present in a Shakespearean masked ball, which is where he would rather be. He isn't in costume yet and he feels out of sorts. He wishes he hadn't arrived so early, so un-dressed, so out of character. Henry might not know it yet but he will have to be the host, because he always is, even though he's never met and will never meet his co-hostess. There's a chair for him to use for the purpose, a seigneurial seat in carved mahogany. It's me who's casting director here, in this summary withdrawal of family ties (or am I rather confirming them?). A director likes to maintain the illusion of control. I'll show them.

I'm reminded of another party, in another imaginary house, a shared birthday for Nora and Dora Chance and Melchior Hazard in *Wise Children*. Like Henry will be this evening when he's changed his clothes, Melchior appears, ancient and resplendent in a costume of majestic kaftan and regal baubles. Henry, from a less informal era, will dress in a dinner jacket for the evening with only a small toque to indicate his role at this and every occasion. Nora's in love and so am I, in love with the idea of being at my mum's party. The burst of joy I feel on realizing that this is where I am and what it means is like endless fireworks. There is, there can be, nothing I want more than this. Nora's in love with her father, who never recognizes her and her twin sister as his children but casts them in productions and invites them to parties in lieu. I must be in love with my dad too, even though I'm not a little girl any more. Those are the reasons why I won't let him be here. My little girl image of him has been put back together; it's not mended.

My mum, brother and I are busy discussing, organizing, deciding, delegating, meeting, ordering. People are coming and going at our bidding and they are actually doing the work. And I'm very very happy to be with my mum. This excitement isn't only about a party. She's here. And I'm here, with her. It's about being with her at all; being with her when I'm not a child any more; seeing her in charge of this event from which (and this means I must be a grown up, doesn't it?) she has apparently allowed me to exclude and invite people as I please, according to my whim. Then I have to go out to buy tobacco: I need cigarettes to suck up some of this emotion. I baulk at sending someone to do it for me and this is not corner shop territory so I leave in pursuit of fags. When I try to come back to the party, I realize I've lost it. I can't get back in. I don't know where it is anymore. I could have been a grown up or a teenager at least with my mum at a party and I left her behind for the sake of roll-ups. Somehow I have to make this blackest of humors add to my pleasure. It's forever a bittersweet, wry regret. I could have stayed with my mum and I chose cigarettes. I could have had her back. This has never happened before, my mum and me, and I wonder why it has happened now, why there in that unreal building, in that unreal place. And I find myself stamping footwear that can't belong to me. It must be a costume party after all. Who did I come as?

• • •

She didn't know what the age difference was between Antony and Fred or who Fred's father was or whether either of their fathers treated them both as sons or how brotherly they were growing up together. Assuming they did grow up together, something else she didn't know. How would she? Placed firmly on one side of two sets of half brothers: she's at one remove on the other side. There's no relation at all except one of proximity. Just like she doesn't know why Fred went to live on the other side of the world in Seattle, when Ant stayed at home for a lifetime with his mum.

There's so much Fred could tell her, so many questions she could ask him. She said, didn't she, that it must have been 20 years since she'd last seen Ant, and in that time she spoke to him only once as far as she could remember. She didn't even know that he had been ill, but there's no reason why she would have known that either. She didn't remember him turning up at any funerals or other family occasions, always away on tour, one way or another. The conversation she had with Fred on the day after the funeral was the first of another flurry of phone calls. They had one of those slightly breathy, crazed exchanges, hopped up with shock. The house at Ennerdale Drive is already on the market, he tells her, and he goes back home to the States in a few days. 'So how are you?' he asks. To which the only answer to almost anyone, is 'Fine.' He sounded strenuously positive in a trans-Atlantic kind of way. Funeral talk. It must be the adrenaline. He invited her to stay if she was ever in New York, where he lives now; repeating the same offer he'd made earlier to her brother, to make sure she understood the offer included her too. He wanted them to know that he really means it, that this wasn't just funeral talk to be forgotten as the grief wore away.

It's a conversation of a formal intimacy that probably captures exactly their non-relationship of not-quite connection and no contact. Fred is strange and slightly familiar. They know and don't know things in common, they are connected to some of the same people but not related. She wonders how it would change the situation if he was someone closer; whether his distance in fact brings advantages and helpful perspective. She wonders if this almost-stranger knows too much or too little. The stranger is owed courtesy and curiosity at least, shelter and the distance of privacy. They gave each other that much.

She remembers how his own family of wife and three children presented as such a bizarrely 'normal' construct 40-odd years ago when they came to stay. Introducing another family into the mix changes everything. Perhaps the distance, the getting away, was the attraction for him. Fred returned to England again about a year after the funeral to complete the sale and pack up the contents of no.2 Ennerdale Drive. Can it really have taken that long to sell? He called her again that time and they had a more measured, relaxed conversation. This time it was as though she knew him, he wasn't a stranger even if he wasn't familiar either. The familiar has to remain strange in some ways, sometimes, to avoid being overlooked and too easily dull. He told her a couple of stories featuring his brother Antony, his brother's brother

Richard and his daughter. That would be herself. It was sweet, like getting presents; a taste of the kind of stories she had hoped to get from Ant. She packed them away for future use, when she came across them again.

What if she could ask Fred the questions?

Why did they buy the house there? Why did his great aunts buy the house new? Why did they buy it together? Why there? Did one of them really go travelling and the other stay home and play house? Why did they leave it to their niece? Really? What was Colindale like when he was growing up? Did Henry come often to Ennerdale Drive? Did Ant go and visit him? Did Fred go too? Why Seattle? What was uncle Ant's life about? Is that right!? And what about his mother's? How many of Fred's half-brother's other half-siblings did he meet when he was growing up? Did Henry and Ant play cricket together? Was Ant's Lothario act a front for being gay? Why did they stay in the house? Why did he go so far to live and Ant stay put in London? And what and how and who?? What do you mean? How did that happen? What?? Tell me tell me tell me.

Even if she could ask the questions, and even if answers were forthcoming, it's never the right information, for all the sweet stories. Something to hold around your heart but nothing there to answer any questions except possibly those forever unformulated. Both times that she spoke to him, after the funeral and after the sale of the house, she still hadn't realized what she needed to ask, or worked out what she needed to know. Which is that the questions are one thing, but that the questions can never be the right ones, never keep you warm enough, never slake the thirst. It's like the archive all over again. By the time she thinks she knows what she needs to ask, he's back across the Atlantic which seems as wide and lengthy to cross as it would have done for transatlantic passengers like Bettina/Bijou/Pam. He's long gone, it turns out, beyond any questions. There's still a few phonecalls to go.

One of her brothers suspected that Fred had not contacted various family members in time for the funeral because he didn't want them to be there. His suspicions involved an imagined trove of Dr Who memorabilia, as if he thought there might be a car boot sale at the crematorium, as if Fred would have the whole lot bundled up into his coat and we'd see it spilling out. But Fred had after all called the last number he could find for her brother. Her brother's skepticism is based perhaps on a fear of the outsider and of being the outsider whose phone number nobody knows; wanting to make someone else the stranger instead of playing it himself. She'd like to be able to prove him wrong, to say to him, 'See?' She doesn't for a moment imagine her brother would have gone to the funeral, but he, and they, would have had the choice. A 70-year-old man whose brother has died after a long illness has to travel from New York to London to arrange the funeral, attend to the usual flotsam of death. These two brothers share a mother only but at least one phone number for an unshared paternal family member can be found in the address book. By the time the call comes round to her, it's very short notice, almost none, for the funeral. So what's the story? And yet, it is strange. But why would Fred do that? Because he wanted to make the funeral as small as possible? And is it any more strange than not seeing your uncle for 20 years?

It could be that her brother was expressing a need for some of that family home stuff, a central hub, a nucleus. It can look good from the outside, especially if you've had nothing of the sort for 40 years. 2 Ennerdale Drive might have been a beacon in Ant's life, a fixed point in a world of performance surrounded by shifting stages, and some of that could be passed on, surely. No wonder all their family connections are shorting. It's easy to see the distance being replicated with families in different continents, countries, regions, planets; with hostilities and/or indifference. None of the distances are really very lengthy but too far to go. The list of what's been lost gets longer: voices necklaces parents addresses pictures connections endings papers. The center is lacking and so is the pivotal figure, the patriarch or matriarch, who makes it all hang together, or who at least makes it look as though it does. This is a role some of those Ainleys would have excelled at, doubtless, given previous similar parts. It doesn't matter whether they're good at it or not; it's all about presence, literal and metaphorical. Being 'good' in this role isn't the point. It's having someone in the role that counts, someone who will turn up and sit it out.

Go and stay with him, like he offered more than once. It's got to be worth a trip to New York to be able to ask. Ask him whatever you want. Ask him all the questions you couldn't ask his brother, all the questions Ant might have told Fred the answers to that he would never have told you. Pick up the phone, ask him. Fred exists, he's alive. Pick up the phone, he might be in.

She tried to call Fred to ask him the questions on the number he'd given her after the funeral. She really did. She made two phone calls to two numbers. She got one number from The Sis. The other was the number that he'd been very keen to give to her in case she was in New York. It was a wrong number and so was the number he'd given to her sister. It's all true then. What she had dismissed as uncharitable pessimism was true. Maybe the Dr Who legacy had existed and had disappeared swiftly from eBay or some classy theatrical ephemera sale, take your pick, with private bids way over expected prices. Maybe Fred enacted some kind of grief-warped funeral charade of making gestures at family connection and making calls too late but being heard to have made them. But that other heightened-through-scarcity, loaded-with-infrequency stuff, like the repeated invitations, she couldn't work out what that was all about.

Fred may have never answered any of the questions but it's never been about being able to get the answers, not really. She has to keep reminding herself that. The missing information about the relationships and childhoods is a kind of impetus. It strengthens, not undermines the framework, as a contrary backbone. Fred did give her what she needed, the house at 2 Ennerdale Drive as portal into a book and an unauthorized voice. Without him, she wouldn't have heard about Ennerdale Drive, and without the story about the house, none of the rest could have existed. The questions left over about where we come from and what our lives sound like are always bigger than those answered. The obvious place to look if she still wanted to shore herself up against the uncertainty of this story is in Colindale. The answer is to go to an archive and pretend to look for artifacts of explanation and to go to the house and look for storylines. The fascination of the house as site of performance is that its existence is certain, even now. The dates are simple and verifiable. It may be crumbling inside and out but it's there to project on to it all sorts of stories. The built object validates the enterprise: it's outside, brick not blood. It's not her. Taking refuge in buildings, is she? I'm not telling. Maybe the archive itself is an artifact of explanation, if you want it to be. Then it might be time for another visit to the Newspaper Library, possibly followed by the London Metropolitan Archive since redrawn borough boundaries in Brent nor Barnet mean that neither borough holds anything relevant. So that's what she does. She combines the visit to the Newspaper Library with a trip to Ennerdale Drive. Always finding what she's never looking for, still.

Here she is again, looking for clues, or something. Not much more than a year after her first visit, she's back on the Northern line, looking for the end of the story in the same place she found the beginning, again peering in at the backs of the houses and going with the familiar roll of the train as it emerges from the tunnel and the underground becomes the overground. The tube line cuts a path between the Police Training Centre at Hendon and the back of the Newspaper Library, a view that shows the building off to great effect with its rows of vertical light apertures interspersed with downpipes running the length of its five stories. Colindale's landmark is being closed down and by the end of 2012 the site occupied by the library and its antecedents for more than a century will be given over to social housing. The newspapers will be rehomed in a new storage facility in Yorkshire, designed to prolong the life of a supposedly endangered but nonetheless proliferating medium through the use of optimum humidity, temperature and oxygen levels.

Before she goes to Ennerdale Drive she walks the opposite way from Colindale station, round to Aeroville. She wants to see if Grahame White's housing is still there to go with the name. Looking at the *London A–Z* has shown her that the whole area between Grahame Park and Colindale is a driving instructor's paradise, endless little roads in loops and cul-de-sacs. The privacy and quiet breeds lifeless hiding places where three-point turns and emergency stops can be practiced undisturbed, where anything can be practiced undisturbed. The silent scream of the suburbs: it's proof of the effects of this kind of neighborhood layout. Aeroville is still standing. More than a name, less than the 'ville' she was expecting, though the name was obviously a source of pride, embossed in the masonry opposite the entranceway, below the flat in prime position, and the only one with French windows. It's a small three-storey estate, laid out as a quadrangle with the road cutting into one side, rather than the street grid of terraced housing she'd assumed. The local council must have taken over its management at some point. In the glass-covered notice board are details about rubbish collection days and tenants' right to buy. The usual warning signs stipulate residents-only parking and forbid ball games. Aeroville's a neat quad but it hasn't been maintained too well recently. Its days of residents' spick-and-span proprietorial, collective pride in this gem of public housing have been replaced with an air of resigned neglect. Like a country town, snickets and paths snake around and across the landscape presenting alternative views of cracked pebbledash and overgrown gardens behind the public face, round the back.

Last time she came here it was spring and the lack of blossom was dismaying; now it's summer and the flowers are doing better. Geraniums and lilies have soaked up recent heavy rain and not been too battered by it. To reach Ennerdale Drive, a shortcut to the high street takes her across a patch of green space, along a path running parallel with the tube line. Wet in the air but no rain yet, she could sit on one of benches shaded by a bower of overgrown branches. It was a mistake to walk this way, the long way round. Heavy, hot clouds make this hard going. But this route goes across Colindeep Lane, named after the original hamlet and she can see the Silk Stream, a weir built in 1928. No one's bothering to top up the suburban-perennial hydrangeas and without an acid or alkali nudge they flower in an indeterminate hue, too wacked-out to be seriously pink or blue. Buddleia sprouts everywhere. These houses are semi-detached too, like Ennerdale Drive; ponderous and somehow insubstantial. There's not much in the way of defensible space and precious little space at all. A Polish food shop has opened on the parade and generally in Colindale revisited the number of cafes has grown, lots of them pitched somewhere between takeaways and fast-food outlets with a few seats.

At the house she sees how the world has turned. It visibly belongs to someone else. 2 Ennerdale Drive now exists only on paper, already only exists in different versions. The changes start with new double back doors which have been inserted in the hedge that runs the length of the garden. It's a small enough innovation, but wide enough to back a car in through the gap. Round the edge of the door frame she can peer into the garden to see children's toys sitting on trimmed grass, a patio of decking with a swing seat and a Japanese acer tree in a big pot in the center. It's all neat and new. She can't knock on the door, there's no point any more.

Signs of the previous occupant have been wiped away at the front of the house, ready for a new chapter. The front garden has been sleekly laid as a driveway with guide lights set into the paving. Parked up on it is a new people carrier. What's left of the hedge is trimmed short so neither view nor access is limited, in and out. They haven't yet replaced the front door, but Ant's sign has been taken down. A lantern is fixed by the side of the door next to a standard bay tree. The metal-framed windows have given way to uPVC double-glazed units, the badly hung dank curtains replaced by blinds. She could suppose Ennerdale Drive to be the same house as long as the metal windows and the hedges and Ant's sign were still in place. Young children couldn't have lived in the house as she had it. Very little of Henry and Bijou's Chart Court survives either. Both houses exist only as imaginary now. And she rattles the knocker after all. They're in but nobody's home. The physical signs that this is a house where people she doesn't know live don't stop her hanging around like a stalker, still determinedly looking for something that isn't there. No wonder they don't want to open the door, she might want to talk to the police in their position.

Copper beech trees are planted in the gaps between the pavement slabs and silver birches across the road. Finally she can hear something: the chatter from a school playground, and birds. She watches some people coming round the corner with shopping in carrier bags to see if they go into no.2. When she crosses the street to get a longer view she sees that a Community Policeman was behind her while she was following potential residents. He goes past the house then turns back and looks across at her, now perched on the garden wall of no.1, writing in a notebook. It's not a crime and he's not a detective either. He looks around for something, then moves away and continues striding slowly up the slope of Ennerdale Drive. The rain starts to fall, as though giving her the permission she needs to leave it behind too. And she does need it. It's all so unmoving.

In the spirit of revised stories and updated archives she planned to ask her sister again for Fred's number, just to check. Her sister gets there first, again, asking whether she has spoken to Fred, and she has to say that the number is wrong, that it isn't his. They check it together. The mistake is obvious immediately. It's the right number written in the wrong order. They had managed to transpose two digits. It's their discrepancy, not his. It's old age, it's dyslexia, it's grief. It's a mistake. She had written down the wrong number in the space of that feverish post-funeral conversation, and her sister had done likewise. It's *As You Like It* all over again: the lost refound and the hidden re-emerging, and someone left looking foolish. Sometime, she might get around to telling her brother.

She went back to Colindale for the end of the story. All the questions she'd like to ask Fred. Still. He started it, he'll have answers, won't he. He started it, he handed her the story, so he can finish.

Epilogue

This is the one. This is that one picture of me with my dad, the single photograph of us to go with the single photograph of the two brothers, Ant and Richard. There's no doubt here: this is me and him. Look at us! It wasn't so hard to find, not too hard to find something when I'm the one choosing both the categories and the hiding places.

And only then I remember: it's me and my dad in the picture and it's me who made the picture too. I said it's one of my favorites, that's because I made it. I made it into what I wanted, as far as I could go before Photoshop. I cut it up. Simple. It gets to be a habit. I decide who goes to the party and I decide who's in the picture. It shows everything I want the world to know about me and my dad. I'd somehow forgotten that had to mean there's a whole lot I didn't want the world to know. I can almost write myself into feeling his arm holding me up around the waist, and how big and strong and secure and forever that felt. It's less a breaking apart of my little girl memories than a confession of my own hand in the making of them. Now I can feel the pasting over of that impression as if I am the photograph. It's like a shock. My revisionist editorial imaging is only part of it; it's all been cracked open otherwise. And that's a whole other story, or maybe this is it.

At the time, all I wanted was a picture of me and my lovely dad, dammit. Mine mine mine. Just us, so that I could imagine I was more than one of three orbiting satellites. I wanted us, no one else. At the time of the Kodak Instamatic I was the one in front of it and him behind. It wasn't even a few pictures of us two alone, it's none and I wanted one at least. I figured that my brothers had enough exposure in thousands of $2^3/_8$ inch-square prints taken before I arrived, so I thought I could take this image and remake this story, recreate this particular moment to suit all my needs. This is what all photographs do, I know, reconstruct real memories in real or imagined spaces, in fictional timespaces. I've turned it around: a fiction constructed in a real space. I might not be the detective but I've tracked myself down. Who's the guilty party now?

The lies and comforts of pictures. I'm getting there. I need to hold the illusion that he was mine, while bearing the knowledge that he was short-term, time-share dad. It doesn't change it after all. That's still me and him there in the spotlight where I've placed us. I wanted to keep hold of the seven-year-old's version, with no other interventions. When you're young you do think things are going to last forever. I know there are other stories now. These are other strands and they coil up together somehow. I know some of them and some of them I don't like and I don't want to know. They don't block each other out.

I cropped it, discarded the rest of the family even though it's one of very few of the family together. I cut them off: my mum and my two brothers. It looks as though I think I can get rid of any of them when I feel like it. I was at it then too, trying to control something that will never be mine. I can't really afford to be so cavalier in my picture editing, but I could say that I made them absent because they are absent. So why not? My family, why shouldn't I? My need for a 'whole family' picture may be great, possibly even too overwhelming to be admitted to, or to imagine fulfilled. The state of the family means that reconstructing the pieces, the sections and slices of family can be more desirable because more achievable in the imaginary and in the image. Unlike the dream of my mum's party, this time I will fix it right. I will imprint a permanent version that I can always return to and that will never be damaged or lost. These are my thoughts as I concentrate on this picture. And that the process of making and remaking is as it should be. I'm still the director here, but I'm very much a player in this tableau and somehow at my own mercy in the end, caught in the plot myself, resisting my own stories. I can't even remember my own moves. Some detective. There are so many layers in this little tale, one that I originally thought brought a wry-edged ending to the bigger story, that I've caught myself out. I can't quite either show or hide all I want to.

It's one of my favorite pictures. It still is. My dad is dangling me-the-toddler on his lap. I'm wearing that 'Look at me and my dad! Aren't I clever?' expression. He's huge, clasping me effortlessly about the middle with his 'good' arm as though I'm a soft toy. He holds me securely, nonchalantly, because it's nothing unusual. He does it all the time. His hand is larger than my face. It's around 1963.

We spent plenty of time together during the day before I went to school and at that time that earned us plenty of attention, which I think both of us enjoyed. I did, a little beam in my big dad's orbit. He cut something of a figure and he liked to stop and talk. In photographs he often looks as though he's reciting lines. Couldn't get him off the stage either, just like his dad. And after I started school he often used to take me there in the morning and walk me back again in the afternoon. He worked at home quite a lot, and was probably at home not working quite a lot too. That's what actors do.

It looks like I'm leaning back into his chest, my head tucked into the crook of his neck, his chin appearing to rest on top of my head. Maybe it's because he has to crane his neck over the top of my head that his gaze looks unfocused, just 'over there'. His left ('bad') arm would be resting on his leg, possibly beneath my left leg but there's a pub-garden table, really a glorified parasol stand, blocking the view. It's out of season so no umbrella is necessary in that flat light. The thin metal disk of the table slices us horizontally, cuts me off above the knees, revealing the end of one trouser leg and two feet in white socks. The plinth cuts my dad vertically along the left shoulder. I wonder who composed this picture so badly, with the table in the foreground. Whoever it was would have used the Instamatic, about the size and shape and weight of a half-pound of butter. 'Don't forget to wind it on', someone would always say, although you couldn't forget because if you hadn't wound it on, the mechanism wouldn't allow you to depress the shutter button the next time. While the film was being advanced the camera gave a satisfying mechanical sound, pleasingly climaxing as the requisite number of sprockets was passed through.

My dad is decked out in his usual old-fashioned American-guy outfit. He lived there during the 1930s and 1940s, became a US citizen, joined the army and returned to England after the war. He's wearing a pale open-weave linen jacket over a plaid shirt, top button done up and peg-top pants made with a noticeable abundance of material compared to English trousers, which were still produced in meaner-cut postwar style. His clothes made him stand out, as did his size and the obvious paralysis, the 'bad' leg etc. The horn-rim glasses are of a distinctly 'American lefty intellectual' style, very Arthur Miller. They are hardly yet somehow significantly different from 1950s NHS. He doesn't have much hair left but it hasn't gone white yet. He's wearing sandals with socks, T-bars with filleted cut-outs around the toes. Still seen on steadfastly unmodern men, with the socks and the glasses. They are almost exactly the same as the ox-blood summer sandals with a punched-out pattern on the toe which children wore to school before trainers and the 1980s.

Along with the trousers, which look too big, I'm kitted out in a stripey t-shirt. Both items were probably cast-offs that had already been through one or both brothers. I had girlish clothes too for trips to dress-wearing places like parties but mostly I was happy looking like my brothers. I had the same haircut as them too. It wasn't meant as a big statement about anything. There's nothing that says 'girl' about my clothes in this picture. I discovered that girls didn't wear string vests only when I started going to school. This is the early 1960s so any ideas of unisex dressing were a good few years off, if unisex ever really happened.

Without the original in front of me I would have assumed this picture was shot on Kodacolour, processed at the chemist round the corner from our house. But no, I find it was black and white, its border yellowing now, printed on Kodak Velox paper, which was available until the 1980s. When I remade the picture in the 1990s I printed it on a heavier matt paper, which somehow removes it further from its context. It's A7, a half-postcard size that I liked then. It's a rich matt but one that still flattens the image, which I suppose is a dimensional rendering of my excision of the rest of the image, deleting my mum and brothers.

So I owe the photographer, whoever he was, gratitude for this witness of the completeness of the family. I say 'he', even though I have no idea who it was. My guess would be a passer-by, someone none of us knew who was pleased enough to be asked to interrupt their day to stand in front of us and ask us to say cheese and press the shutter. Or the waiter in the café where we're sitting. Take our order, take our picture. Thank you so much. But that's not it. It was someone we all knew very well indeed then, later to be lost and refound along with so much else. I only had to crop out one brother. That leaves one more to be present to take the picture. In the original composition the family group is positioned slightly to the right, the French windows behind us pleasingly off-center. The parasol table in the foreground is my fault, the cost of my remake. It neatly quarters the image, there in front of us. The bottom left and right are a mess of legs: table, chair, my dad's; the wall of the building, his left shoulder and arm fill the top right; my dad's head and torso and most of me take up top left. Now I've realized and now you know, the crop is so obvious and so bad I might as well have torn the picture up and left the edges ragged or scribbled over the other faces. There is no format like this. I didn't even try to cover my tracks. I could have put a white border around it at least to lend some authority to my butchery or rebuilt the picture to make it a recognizable size. Look at that daddy's girl! Everything I want the world to know about my dad is contained in this image, and this composition is the entirety of the narrative I will share. So I thought.

That's what I wanted to think, anyway. Looking more closely, I can see how far I've struggled to fantasize with the power of reversal. My dad looks tired. That's what comes of having a tubby four-year-old on your knee and being a 50-something father of three young children. Maybe his wrecked body meant he was always tired, or his medication sapped him, or maybe it didn't work properly so he's worn out from pain, just like the man said. Perhaps he just didn't sleep well the night before in a hotel bed. His mouth is stretched wide open, he was in the middle of speaking or yawning. I must have been focusing only on the comfort of his bulk, on the way he's holding me, which in turn encapsulates something I strive to maintain about the enduring security his figure represents to me. I did want to hold on to that. Except that in a multitude of ways, it's only part of the story. There's too much for me to know here too.

The image has currency for me on two levels. There's the idealization of my relationship with my dad. Never mind that it turns out there is nothing much about this last exhibit, this photographic (or other) evidence to corroborate my version, except to confirm again that a photograph recalls what is absent from it and that the reading is all. The photograph allows an unresolved past to surface; it is the surface only. This image and the narratives it disrupts are what remains of the memory, it is the 'fossil of what has been forgotten' as Laura Marks describes it. Then there's the Ainley family on holiday on the south coast sitting outside a hotel, waiting for a cup of tea to arrive. I rework my dad into the being I want him to be. And I almost get there. I can keep quiet about everything else that I don't want to tell the world about him.

Bibliography

Tudor Walters Report. (1918).

Smart A. (editor). (1999). *London Suburbs*. London, Merrell and English Heritage.

Agam, P (1988) Interwar suburbia: the appearance of English suburban housing built between 1919 and 1939 as typified by the suburbs of north-west London. Research Award report held at RIBA British Architectural Library, V&A Museum

Agamben, G. (2007). *Profanations*. New York, Zone Books.

Bachelard, G. (1994). *The Poetics of Space*. Boston, UK, Beacon.

Bal, M. editor. (1994). *The Point of Theory: Practices of cultural analysis*. Amsterdam, University of Amsterdam Press.

Barber, S. (1995). *Fragments of the European City*. London, Reaktion.

Barthes, R. (1977). *Image Music Text*. London, Fontana.

Barthes, R. (2000). *Camera Lucida*. London, Vintage.

Barthes, R. (2000). *Mythologies*. London, Vintage.

Benjamin, W. (1999). 'The Storyteller' in *Illuminations*. London, Pimlico.

Benjamin, W. (1999). 'Theses on the Philosophy of History' in *Illuminations*. London, Pimlico.

Benjamin, W. (2006). *Berlin Childhood around 1900*. Cambridge, Mass., Belknap Harvard University Press.

Benjamin, W. (1996). *The Arcades Project*. Cambridge, Mass and London, Belknap/Harvard.

Berger, J. (1991). *About Looking*. New York, Vintage.

Bergson, H. (1991). *Matter and Memory*. New York, Zone Books.

Borges, J. L. (2007). *Labyrinths*. New York. W. W. Norton & Co.

Boyd, W. (2006). *Restless*. London, Bloomsbury.

Bracewell, M. (1997) *England is mine: pop life in Albion from Wilde to Goldie*. HarperCollins. London.

Brown, S. (1996). *Bristol Old Vic Theatre School 1946–1996*. Bristol,

BOVTS Productions.

Bruno, G. (2002). *Atlas of Emotion*. New York, Verso.

Bruno, G. (2007). *Public Intimacy: Architecture and the Visual Arts*. Cambridge, Mass. And London. MIT Press.

Buck-Morss, S. (1989). *The Dialectic of Seeing*. Cambridge, Mass. and London, MIT Press.

Burnett, J. (1980). *A Social History of Housing 1815–1970*. Methuen. London

Busch, A. (1999). *Geography of Home*. Princeton Architectural Press. New York

Calvino, I. (1997). *Invisible Cities*, Vintage.

Calvino, I. (1996). *Six Memos for the Millennium*. Vintage. London.

Carr, C and Whitehand, J. (2001). *Twentieth-Century Suburbs*, Routledge.

Carter, A. (1991). *Wise Children*. London, Chatto & Windus.

Certeau, M. (1988). *The Practice of Everyday Life*. Berkeley, University of California Press.

Citron, M. (1999). *Home Movies and other Necessary Fictions*. Minneapolis/London, University of Minnesota Press.

Clarke, K. (2007). 'Two minds: Artists and Architects in Collaboration', Jes Fernie, ed.

Cochran, C. B. (1945). *Showman looks on*. London, JM Dent & Sons Ltd.

Colomina, B. (editor). (1992). *Sexuality and Space*. Princeton Architectural Press. New York

Colomina, B. (1996). *Privacy and Publicity*. Cambridge, Mass. And London. MIT Press.

Colomina, B. (2002). Architectureproduction. *This is not architecture*. K. Rattenbury. London/NY, Routledge.

Colomina, B. (2006). *Serpentine pavilion talks*.

Colomina, B. (1990). 'Intimacy and Spectacle: The Interiors of Adolf Loos.' *AA Files* 20.

Connah, R. (1989). *Writing Architecture: Fantomas Fragments Fictions, An Architectural Journey through the 20th Century*.

Cambridge, Mass. and London, MIT Press.

Crossan, M. editor. (2006). *Tales from Ten Cities.* ???, Comma Press.

Czinner, P. director (1936). As You Like It. England: 92 mins.

Davidson, R. (2006) Laing accepts £886.9m takeover bid in Guardian Unlimited 19/9/2006

Derrida, J. (1987). *The Postcard: From Socrates to Freud and beyond.* Chicago, University of Chicago Press.

Derrida, J. (1996). *Archive Fever: A Freudian Impression.* Chicago and London, University of Chicago.

Dillon, B. (2006). *In the Darkroom: A Journey in Memory.* 2006, Penguin.

Douglas, M. (1988). *Purity and Danger.* London, Routledge.

Edwards, A. (1981). *The Design on Suburbia: A Critical Study in Environmental History.* London, Pembridge Press.

Evans, R. (1997). *Translations from Drawing to Building and other essays.* London, AA Publications.

Forded, B. (1989). *The Edwardian Age and the Inter-War Years,* Cambridge University Press.

Foucault, M. (1991). *The Birth of the Clinic: An Archaeology of Medical Perception.* London, Routledge.

Freud, S. (2003). Remembering, Repeating and Working Through. *Beyond the Pleasure Principle and Other Writings.* London, Penguin.

Freud, S. (2003). On dreams. *Beyond the Pleasure Principle and Other Writings.* London, Penguin.

Gibson, J. K. A. editor. (2003). *London from Punk to Blair,* Reaktion.

Giddens, A. (1991). *Modernity and Self-Identity.* Cambridge, Polity Press.

Grosz, E. (2001). *Architecture from the Outside: Essays on Virtual and Real spaces.* Cambridge, Mass, MIT Press.

Gunn, E. (1932). *Economy in House Design.* London, Architectural Press.

Gunning, T. (2003). 'The Exterior as Intérieur: Benjamin's Optical

Detective'. *Boundary* 2 (Spring 2003).

Hall, K. (2007). *The Stuff of Dreams: Fantasy, Anxiety and Psychoanalysis*. London, Karnak.

Hanley, L. (2007). *Estates: an intimate history*, Granta Books

Hardie, E. (n.d.). *Henry Ainley: Portrait of a Great Actor*. unpublished manuscript

Hendon, Z. (2007). Transcript of talk, *Designed for you*, Turner Contemporary, Margate.

Hillier, B. (2004). *Betjeman: The Bonus of Laughter*, John Murray.

HMSO (1927). Housing Manual on the Design Construction and Repair of Dwellings. Ministry of Housing. Foreword by Neville Chamberlain, HMSO.

Hoffman, E. *The Sandman*. download, Virginia Commonwealth University, 1994–1999 Robert Godwin-Jones

Hornsby, L. editor. (1938). *The Complete Guide to Homemaking: Home Owner's Handbook*. London, Shaw Publishing.

Housman, A. A Shropshire Lad.

Hughes, F. editor. (1996) *The Architect Reconstructing her Practice*. MIT, Boston.

Hutten, B. v. (1905) *Pam*. AL Burt Company. New York

Hutten, B. v. (1923). *Pam at Fifty*. London, New York, Toronto, Melbourne, Cassell.

Hutten, B. v. (1931). *Pam's Own Story*. Philadelphia and London, Lippincott.

Inquiry, I. o. (2007). *Searching for Sebald: Photography after Sebald*. LA, Institute of Inquiry

Jack, I. (2006). 'Introduction to Loved Ones'. *Granta* 95.

Jackson, A. A. (1973). *Semidetached London*, Allen + Unwin.

Jones, O. (2005). 'An Ecology of Emotion, Memory, Self and Landscape' in *Emotional Geographies*. L. B. Joyce Davidson, Mick Smith. Hampshire, UK and Vermont, USA.

Kahn, N. (2004). *My Architect*. US: 116 minutes.

Kidder, T. (1999) *House*. Boston/New York. Mariner Books

Kuhn, A. (1995). *Family Secrets*. London, New York, Verso.

Laing, R. (1971). *The Politics of the Family and Other Essays*. London, Tavistock.

Littlefield, D. and Lewis, S. (2007). *Architectural Voices: Listening to Old Buildings*. Chichester, Wiley-Academy.

MacManus, D. (1986). Little Palaces. *King of America*, F Beat Records.

Mansfield, J. (1923). *The House We Ought to Live in*. London, Duckworth.

Marker, C. (2002). *Immemory*, Exact Change. CD-ROM

Marker, C. director. (1983). *Sans Soleil*. France

Marks, L. (2000). *The Skin of the Film: Intercultural cinema, Embodiment and the senses*. Durham and London, Duke University Press

McCarthy, Tom. (2006) *Remainder*, London, Alma Books

Melville, J. (1997) *Ellen Terry and Smallhythe Place*. National Trust, Swindon

Michaels, A. (1998). *Fugitive Pieces*. London, Bloomsbury.

Mirzoff, E. (1973). Metro-Land.

MoDA. (2003). Mark Pinner et al *Little Palaces: House and home in the interwar suburbs*. London, Middlesex University Press.

Moretti, F. (1983). *Signs Taken for Wonders: Essays on the Sociology of Literary Forms*. London, Verso/NLB.

Morris, P., editor. (1997). *The Bakhtin Reader: Selected writings of Bakhtin, Medvedev, Volshinov*. London: Arnold.

Morris, S. (2000). 'Turning a Telescope on the Soul: Freud's Interpretation of the Structure of the Psyche' in *Drawing the Soul: Schemas and Models in Psychoanalysis*. B. Burgoyne. London, Rebus Press.

Morris, S. (2000). *Shifting Eyes*. London, University College, London. PhD.

Mulvey, L. (1989). 'Melodrama inside and outside the home' in *Visual and other pleasures*. London, MacMillan.

Nabokov, V. (2000). *Speak, Memory: An Autobiography Revisited*. London Penguin Modern Classics

Newton, W. G. (1925). *Prelude to Architecture.* London, Architectural Press.

Nobus, D. (2000). 'Who am I?' in *The Ego and the Self in Psychoanalysis.* B. Seu. London Rebus Press.

Oliver, P., Davis, I., Bentley, I. (1981). *Dunroamin: The Suburban Semi and its Enemies.* London, Barrie & Jenkins.

Pallasmaa, J. (2005). *The Eyes of the Skin: Architecture and the Senses.* Chichester, Wiley-Academy.

Pamuk, O. (2005). *Istanbul,* Faber & Faber.

Pamuk, O. (2007). *My Father's Suitcase,* Route-online.

Perec, G. (1988). *W of The Memory of Childhood.* London. Collins Harvill.

Perec, G. (1999) *Species of Space and Other Pieces* edited and translated by John Sturrock. Penguin Books. London

Philips, A. (1999). *Darwin's worms.* London, Faber + Faber.

Phillips, J. A. (2009) *Lark & Termite.* London, Jonathan Cape

Phillips, J. and Barrett, H. (1988). *Suburban Style: The British home 1840–1988.* London and Sydney, MacDonald Orbis.

Platt, E. (2000). *Leadville: A Biography of the A40,* London. Picador.

Podbury, M. (1997) *Man Half Beast Making a Life in Canadian Theatre.* Montréal. Véhicule Press

Pollock, G. (2009).'The Missing Photograph: Charlotte Salomon Life? Or Theatre as the Encounter with Maternal Loss' in *Reading Life Writing New Formations.* London. Lawrence and Wishart

Powers, A. (2002). 'The Architecture Book' in *This is not architecture.* K. Rattenbury. London/NY, Routledge.

Raynaud, Claudine. (2009) '"Flesh and Blood": Auotobiographical "Material" between Fiction and Non-fiction' in *Reading Life Writing New Formations.* London. Lawrence and Wishart

Read, A. (1993). *Theatre and Everyday Life: An Ethics of Performance.* London, Routledge.

Rendell, J. (2006). *Art and Architecture: A Place Between.* London and New York, IB Tauris.

Ritchie, Berry. (1997). *The Good Builder: The John Laing Story*. London, James & James.

Ronell, A. (1993). *Dictations on Haunted Writing*, University of Nebraska Press.

Ross, C. (2003). *Twenties London: A City in the Jazz Age*, Philip Wilson.

Roth, P. (1988). *The Facts*. US, Vintage.

Rugg, L. H. (1997). *Picturing Ourselves*. Chicago and London, University of Chicago Press.

Russell, C. 'Autoethnography: Journeys of the Self'. excerpt from *Experimental Ethnography*, Duke University Press www.haussite.net>script section

Ryle, Martin (2009) John McGahern: 'Memory, Autobiography, Fiction' in *Reading Life Writing New Formations*. London. Lawrence and Wishart

Samuel, Raphael. (1994) *Theatres of Memory*, Verso London

Sennett, R. (2002). *The Fall of Public Man*. London. Penguin.

Sharp, T. (1945). *Town Planning*. London, Pelican.

Shibli, A. (2003). *Lost Time*. Manchester, Cornerhouse.

Silverstone, R. (1994). *Television and Everyday Life*. London, Routledge.

Stamp, G. (2006). 'Neo-Tudor and its Enemies'. *Architectural History* 45:2006.

Steedman, C. (1986). *Landscape for a good woman: A story of two lives*. London, Virago.

Steedman, C. (1992). *Past Tenses: Essays on writing, autobiography and history*. London. Rivers Oram.

Steedman, C. (2001). *Dust*. Manchester, Manchester University Press.

Steedman, C. (2009). 'On Not Writing Biography' in *Reading Life Writing New Formations*. London. Lawrence and Wishart

Swenarton, M. (1981). *Homes fit for heroes*. London, Heinemann.

Tennyson, A. (1854). The Charge of the Light Brigade.

Todorov, T. (1977). *The Poetics of Prose*. Blackwell. Oxford

Turchi, P. (2004). *Maps of the Imagination: The Writer as Cartographer*. San Antonio, Trinity University Press.

Turkington, R. and Ravetz, A. (1995). *The Place of Home: English Domestic Environments 1914–2000*. London. Chapman + Hall.

unattributed (1935). 'Sunnyfields Estate, Mill Hill: AA Competition in conjunction with Messrs John Laing & Son'. *AA Journal* December pp.253–265.

unattributed (1936). 'The Architect and Housing by the Speculative Builder: Sunnyfields Estate, Mill Hill'. *RIBA Journal*. 18 January 1936

unattributed (1987). *Little Palaces: The Suburban House in North London 1919–1939*, Middlesex Polytechnic.

unattributed (1934). London and Suburb: Old and new, Useful knowledge for Health and Home.

unattributed (1935). *New House*. London. September and October issues.

Vidler, A. (1992). *The Architectural Uncanny*. Cambridge, Mass., MIT Press.

Walsh, F. (2006) Henderson raises bid for Laing in *The Guardian*, 11/11/2006

Walsh, F. (2006) Henderson beats Allianz to John Laing in *The Guardian*, 11/16/2006

Weaver, M. Ideal homes and petty snobberies in *The Guardian*, 28/9/2005

Webster, M. (1969). *Five Generations of a Great Theatre Family: The Same Only Different*, Victor Gollancz Ltd.

Wood, J. (2008). *How Fiction Works*. London, Jonathon Cape.

Woolf, C. (1995). *A Model Childhood*.

Contemporary culture has eliminated both the concept of the public and the figure of the intellectual. Former public spaces – both physical and cultural – are now either derelict or colonized by advertising. A cretinous anti-intellectualism presides, cheerled by expensively educated hacks in the pay of multinational corporations who reassure their bored readers that there is no need to rouse themselves from their interpassive stupor. The informal censorship internalized and propagated by the cultural workers of late capitalism generates a banal conformity that the propaganda chiefs of Stalinism could only ever have dreamt of imposing. Zer0 Books knows that another kind of discourse – intellectual without being academic, popular without being populist – is not only possible: it is already flourishing, in the regions beyond the striplit malls of so-called mass media and the neurotically bureaucratic halls of the academy. Zer0 is committed to the idea of publishing as a making public of the intellectual. It is convinced that in the unthinking, blandly consensual culture in which we live, critical and engaged theoretical reflection is more important than ever before.